"What if this visit didn't end?" he asked.

"What do you mean?"

He'd been thinking this over ever since he had seen AJ and Zaire together, playing carefree. Then whenever Zaire had approached Yusra and asked her to help push him on a swing or rock him on the spring rider toy, she hadn't treated his son differently from her own. He'd caught longing glances from her toward Zaire, her maternal love unhidden and shining in her eyes. She couldn't help it, and she shouldn't have to hide it. He was her son.

Just as AJ was his family.

"Fair warning, it's unorthodox. But it will relieve us from having to choose to walk away."

"Tell me." Conviction carved her demand, and it sparked to life in her. He watched it burn in her coal-dark eyes, add a richer red to her deep brown skin and straighten her posture from the force of it.

"Marriage. If we were to marry, then the children could stay with us both, and the option of having to leave and say farewell becomes moot."

Dear Reader,

A baby swap, a billionaire and a marriage of convenience? Oh my!

But that's everything I jam-packed into *The Baby Swap That Bound Them*.

I love each of these deliciously drama-filled tropes and hooks, and they all play a vital role in bringing Yusra and Bashir together. Because they really are two very different people, and without fate stepping in—in the form of a baby swap *wink*—they would probably never even meet! And we can't have that, right? Right.

In all seriousness, Bashir and Yusra's story is one of hope, healing, and regaining the ability to trust and love. They both have suffered losses in differing ways, which have left them resistant to opening their hearts up to romance. Writing their happily-ever-after was a roller coaster of emotion. I cried, laughed and cheered for them through their ups and downs.

I can't say it was easy, so I won't wish you have the exact same emotional experience, but I do sincerely hope their love story leaves a happy imprint on your heart and mind the way it has mine.

Happy reading always!

Hana

x

The Baby Swap That Bound Them

Hana Sheik

Recycling programs for this product may not exist in your area.

ISBN-13: 978-1-335-73719-9

The Baby Swap That Bound Them

Harlequin Enterprises ULC
22 Adelaide St. West, 41st Floor
Toronto, Ontario M5H 4E3, Canada
www.Harlequin.com

Printed in U.S.A.

Hana Sheik falls in love every day reading her favorite romances and writing her own happily-ever-afters. She's worked various jobs—but never for very long because she's always wanted to be a romance author. Now she gets to happily live that dream. Born in Somalia, she moved to Ottawa, Canada, at a very young age, and still resides there with her family.

Books by Hana Sheik

Harlequin Romance

Second Chance to Wear His Ring
Temptation in Istanbul
Forbidden Kisses with Her Millionaire Boss

Visit the Author Profile page
at Harlequin.com for more titles.

For Kaysim.

The cutest little nephew an aunt could be so lucky to snuggle!

Love you forever and more, Habo.

PROLOGUE

"HE'S SO TINY."

Yusra brushed her fingertips over the back of her son's small curling fist, the peach fuzz soft, his skin warm and flushed red. He mewled in his sleep, shifting toward her at one point. One look and she was smitten. Now she understood what her mother meant when she'd told her that it took only a glance sometimes to fall in love. She'd thought and feared that after her difficult pregnancy and tumultuous, touch-and-go birth she would feel none of the maternal feelings she was meant to experience.

Thankfully all she felt were pure relief and love for the unknowing child in the bassinet.

"Would you like to hold him?" The nurse who'd been tending her guided Yusra to a padded rocking chair by a small picture window. A window that she shared with the two other mothers in the cramped, too warm hospital room. She forgot how stuffy the room could be when the sun angled in through the window and slanted shafts of white light over her hospital bed. Soon as her son was placed in her arms, the sweat beading at the back of her neck, under her armpits and tracking down her spine ceased to be a concern. Because she had everything she needed pressed to her chest and her drumming heart.

"Support his head this way, and make sure his hat doesn't slip off. We don't want him getting too cold."

Yusra smothered the laugh. She didn't think that could happen quickly. Maybe in one of the fancy, private rooms with the temperature control would such a problem exist. Not here. Not in the heated but cozy corner of theirs.

She cuddled her son, instinct driving her to bring him closer to her breast. This was her first time holding him since he'd spent his first two days in the NICU. The short separation made their reunion so much sweeter.

"I didn't think anyone could be so small."

"It might seem that way now, but they grow fast. Faster than you might be prepared for."

Yusra looked up from the small scrunched face of her son, her hand stroking his scalp, fingers lingering on his baby-soft black tufts of hair. He had a headful of the wispy curls, so unlike her own, but reminding her of his father.

Before her throat could get too thick to ask, she wondered, "You have children?"

'Three. The youngest is off to primary school, but it feels like yesterday when I was sitting in the same position that you are." The nurse looked down at the newborn son Yusra had to care for now all on her own. "Did you pick a name?"

"No, not yet. I'm still deciding." Yusra stared down at her son's closed eyes and pursing wet mouth. She caressed his cheek with a finger and marveled at his natural rooting instinct to turn in the direction and seek her breasts. She wasn't nursing fully yet, but she was trying. She didn't want to miss the chance to connect with him on that level if she could.

"Whatever you pick I'm sure will be the perfect choice." Then the nurse moved away to do her rounds. She returned ten minutes later to collect Yusra's son and place him in his bassinet again.

"I'll check your blood sugar and bring dinner over soon."

Being diabetic had erased her fear of needles a long time ago. But she didn't anticipate her heart racing faster when her diabetes was mentioned. She imagined that the trauma she'd suffered only a few days earlier had further repercussions than she believed it would.

"Everything looks good," the nurse reported with a smile. "I know you like the coconut potato soup. I will sneak the one with the most avocado in it for you. And maybe the—"

A long, drawn-out, frightening wail pierced the air and cut off whatever else her assigned nurse was going to say.

The nurse rushed away, leaving Yusra to be grateful that the scream hadn't woken her son. Moving on her own and fast was still a challenge. She lingered sitting on her bed, a hand clasped around the clear-sided bassinet holding her baby boy.

What had happened out there?

She remembered her own perilous birth story. The vivid memories of the sharp uterine pains, the fetal position she'd been in when help arrived in the form of paramedics that a kindly neighbor in her apartment building had called, and the blood, the agonizing, awful pushing and her cries echoing off the walls of her hospital room. She'd thought she would die. She thought she would never see her baby, and no one would care for him the way she did now.

It had been concurrently the worst and best experience of her life.

But the cry she'd heard triggered anxiety in her. It hadn't sounded like a mother giving birth at all. It sounded…

Brushing a kiss on her son's forehead, she wrapped a shawl over her head and followed her gut. It lured her out of bed and her room. She met no resistance in the dimly lit hospital corridor, the nurses too busy attending to the new and expectant mothers on the obstetrics floor to notice her ambling slowly in the direction of the bloodcurdling scream.

She slowed at double doors, but pushed on undeterred. She didn't know why she cared so much. Only that something resonated with her about the pitiful scream. It wasn't long before she noticed this new hospital area was brighter, cleaner and quieter. Also, the bustle she'd left behind was notably missing.

What am I doing? The thought came swiftly and rooted her feet.

She'd left her son to go snoop on another patient, like it was any of her business. Blaming her heightened maternal emotions, she turned to walk away, but stopped when she caught movement in her peripherals.

A shockingly tall, hulking man stepped out of one of the rooms. In his dark business suit, he didn't look like he belonged. And yet he pressed a big hand to the closed door in front of him, his broad shoulders caving in, and his head hanging low. Sorrow or defeat, she didn't know which had crushed him, but her sympathy went out to him. Surviving her own near death and becoming a mother had changed her into this self-reflective being.

Before she could leave him to his private display of emotion, she heard her name.

"Ms. Amin, you shouldn't be here."

It was her duty nurse. She appeared by her side and, gently gripping her arm, swung her back the way she'd come. Though not fast enough. The man looked up and over their way, his eyes and scowl as dark as his suit, long thick beard and short curly hair. With only one glance he communicated what she figured a man like him—a man who probably had the world clutched in his large hand and determined his own fate—would when someone like her tried to infiltrate his controlled bubble. *You're intruding here*, was what she felt his eyes accused her of doing.

And she really was.

Giving in, she allowed herself to be led away, and with no more backward glances.

Once she was in her room, the nurse tucked her in and gently reminded her of the hospital's rules. Listening with half a mind, she focused the other half on her final image of the man grieving outside the hospital room.

"Who was he?" she asked, realizing too late she'd spoken aloud.

She hadn't thought the nurse saw him, but she was proven wrong. "I think I know who you're talking about. I don't know his name, but he's just lost a family member to a terrible car accident."

"No wonder he looked so sad." That didn't explain why he was on this floor though. "Shouldn't he be on the emergency floor?"

The nurse whispered, "I really shouldn't say more." She looked pointedly at Yusra's son, her face softened by sadness. "It's not something a new mother should hear anyways."

"That might be true… Still, I'd like to know. Did someone else get hurt?"

She had an out-of-body sensation, prickling over her arms and legs, and cooling her despite the heat circulating the small hospital room.

Somehow, she knew the answer to that question even before the nurse nodded sadly. "There was also a female victim in the accident. Another family member. She survived the crash but was lost to childbirth. The whole family is grieving together right this moment."

"The baby?" Yusra's mouth dried, her putty-like heart sticking in her throat, chilly desolation seeping into her fast. "Is the baby alive?"

"Yes," the nurse said with a smile.

Releasing a loud, quick breath, relief chased off the emotional cold that had prepared her body for the worst news. At least the child had lived. She'd always hated sad, unpredictable story endings for that reason. She didn't want to cry. Didn't want to wonder why the world was unfair sometimes.

It made her think how close she'd come to that. Leaving her child behind. Losing the life she had dreamed up for the two of them.

That could have been her, the woman who died in childbirth.

When the nurse left to fetch her dinner, Yusra stroked and kissed the hands, cheeks and head of her tiny son. "I swear I'll always fight to stay with you," she vowed.

The heartbreaking story of loss and mourning only several doors away persisted to haunt her until she considered a name for her baby instead. A name that would represent the strong, sunny future she hoped to build for him so that he never felt something was amiss in his life. And while she did that, she almost, *almost* forgot about the scowling, dark-bearded man who suffered levels of untold pain where she had experienced immeasurable joy.

CHAPTER ONE

Two years and nine months later

A SMALL MOTORBOAT sliced across the still ocean, casting a frothing line of water in its wake and disrupting the calm horizon and illusory peace. Nothing about this morning was like any morning Bashir Warsame had experienced since committing to his unorthodox lifestyle. Living on board his seventy-meter superyacht for close to three years, and occasionally anchoring, had dulled his patience for company. Most people who worked for him or with him knew he didn't like face-to-face meetings. He managed his vast international hotel chain from the comfort of his private cabin, and he hadn't found himself missing any part of his existence on land.

And yet someone had missed the memo and was heading full steam ahead toward his ship.

Bashir waited until the boat was close before he walked away. As he made his way aft, he was met by his ship's senior master Nadim and Nadim's ever-present tablet computer. The man didn't go anywhere without it.

"I've briefed your team and ours on the security protocol." Nadim looked up from the screen of his palm-sized tablet, his data and figures and facts meticulously logged and tracked in the portable device. Bashir never questioned Nadim's reliance on it. Whatever he was doing, it was what had kept the crew and ship running smoothly and efficiently, and as far as Bashir was concerned, that was the only thing that mattered.

"Have they made contact yet?"

Nadim repeated the question into his earpiece, shaking his head. "They're boarding now. Security will hold them."

"Handle it. I'll be in the lounge." Nadim had his full trust. He didn't see a reason to interfere in the other man's duties. And he didn't give his confidence to others very easily. But his senior master had more than earned it, in time and service.

Wordlessly, Nadim dipped his chin and at the next junction they parted ways. Nadim toward where security would greet their unwelcome guest, whoever they were, and Bashir to his second most favorite place on his ship: the underwater observation lounge.

He took a deeply satisfying breath before entering the expansive room and again when he claimed the central spot on the smooth leather sofa facing the panoramic ocean view. As always, he let it sink in that very little stood between him and the yawning, hungry maw of the dark blue waters he was observing quietly. Nothing but glass panels. If he were the type to seek thrill from death-defying activities, he'd have thought himself to be entirely safe from the threat that the ocean always posed. He wasn't that naive. Though sometimes...sometimes he wished that he were.

Then he'd be able to close his eyes and finally rid himself of this constant alertness he lived with day in and day out. His vigilance a byproduct of having to fight for where he was today. Because of that, he had more at stake. Naturally, losing everything and everyone he cared for was a perennial thought. And if he wasn't always on guard, then that was when he was most susceptible to losing it all.

Bashir shut his eyes, breathed through his nose and almost attained a semblance of peace— when he snapped his eyes open and turned to the ruckus barging into the lounge.

It happened fast.

The polished oak doors into the room burst open and his toddler son Zaire came rushing in with a mildly harassed albino rabbit gripped in his small pudgy arms. Behind him, hot on his trail and looking more than hot under the collar, was Zaire's overpaid and equally overworked nanny. Bashir grimaced at both the intrusion and out of sympathy for the woman who had to mind his rambunctious son all day. Middle-aged Alcina might not have been the best choice for a toddler who hadn't yet grasped the concept of slowing down, but she'd been Bashir's only choice from the beginning. She'd started out as his housekeeper, back when he had roots on land, and when he had anchored away from his palatial island villa in Greece, Alcina had asked to come along and help him in any way.

Her loyalty was touching, but he supposed she possibly regretted it a bit now.

Alcina stopped fanning her flushed high-boned cheeks, and she stooped to catch his son when he all but launched himself *and* his ruffled pet rabbit into his nanny's open arms. Alcina dropped a kiss on his head and squeezed him to her.

Bashir amended his earlier thought. Clearly, Alcina was a perfect caregiver for his son in more ways than not.

He would've thought that disruption enough. Yet Nadim arriving in the lounge reminded him that there were more distractions ahead of him. Especially when his senior master gave him an uncharacteristic frown.

With puckered brows and a growing scowl, Nadim requested, "May I speak to you?" His eyes passed over Alcina and Zaire. The meaning in them clear as mud. He didn't want an audience for whatever he had to report.

Bashir understood. A final glance at the glass caging the ocean, and he stood to address whatever issue had now fallen onto his lap.

Nadim joined him in his office, a floor directly above the observation deck.

"What is it, man?" he asked soon as he was seated behind his executive desk. It was large and ostentatious, and he hardly ever used the whole space, but it communicated the kind of front his money could afford. Just like the glass in his underwater lounge separating him from the dangers of the waters surrounding them, he kept the world at bay in the same way, one hand always thrust out to discourage anyone getting closer to him.

Nadim and Alcina were the handful in his trusted circle of company.

He didn't make friends easily. And he hadn't had family in a long time.

Shaking off the tendrils of trauma that resurfaced whenever he thought of his long-gone family, he considered the power he now possessed to prevent Zaire from ever experiencing what he'd had to. It was why he appreciated Nadim for his forethought in suggesting their meeting be held elsewhere. His son might be a few months from his third birthday, but Zaire could be uncannily perceptive for a young child who was only beginning to learn his alphabet. There had been the possibility that his son would have sensed something was amiss if Nadim had chosen to deliver his news in the observation lounge. The risk of upsetting Zaire was abolished now that they'd swapped venues.

His senior master passed his ever-handy tablet over. "Do you recognize this woman? She's the one who hired a boat to ferry her to our ship."

The image on the tablet was of an older woman, her skin a fair brown and the bags under her eyes darkly pronounced. She had the lower half of her face, from the nose down, covered by her shawl. Only those haunting eyes gazed out at him. Even through the photo he sensed her desperation. It clawed out at him, grasping at air, and right before it choked him, he flipped the tablet facedown over his desk.

"Who is she?" Rather than admitting he didn't know her and hadn't the faintest clue what connection she had to him, or why and how she'd come to be on his ship.

"A former nurse from the Kampala City International Hospital. She wishes to speak with you and says it has to do with Zaire."

About his son? What could she possibly have to tell him about Zaire?

"Did she say anything more?"

Nadim shook his head, his expression softly speculative. "Only that she won't speak to anyone but you."

Scowling, Bashir furiously sifted his brain on what to do next. Not that he had to think for very long. His options dwindled, soon as he heard his son was involved somehow.

He was sensitive when it came to his child.

Zaire's birth story was tragic. Bashir didn't like ruminating about his family as a rule, mostly as his mind always seemed to veer to its darkest, most depressing corners. But he couldn't stop the memories of the day he'd gotten the call that his cousin Imran had died in a car accident in Kampala, Uganda. Imran's pregnant wife, Tara, had been a victim too. Unlike Imran, she hadn't died at the scene. She'd gone into premature labor and, despite her grievous wounds, she had miraculously delivered a healthy baby boy. As Bashir understood it, Tara had gotten to hold her newborn son for all of a few minutes before she went into hemorrhagic shock, slipped into a coma and never woke up again.

By the time he'd arrived, Tara and Imran were both gone.

Zaire was left alone.

Bashir knew what that loneliness was like. Twenty-eight years ago he'd lost his whole family—grandparents, parents, brothers, and sisters—to a flash flood that had swept through their Somali village. He had been the sole survivor of the tragedy, a confused and frightened seven year old.

Orphaned and homeless all of a sudden Bashir had moved to live with his aunt and uncle, Imran's parents. He hadn't met his cousin or that part of the family before, but he had been raised to respect all family members he encountered, and anticipated a good life with his aunt and uncle and many cousins.

And that was what he'd gotten. His extended family embraced him as if he were one of their own. In spite of their struggles, his uncle's farm bringing only so much food—and seasonal famines to contend with—Bashir never went hungry and was hardly ever exposed to any troubles. His cousins were all around his age, with Imran being the oldest and three years older than Bashir was. And yet their age gap didn't stop them from connecting instantly. Before long, Bashir could almost call Imran a brother. They did everything together. Imran allowed him to tag along to play with his older friends. They studied together. Ate all their meals as a family from one communal plate. Shared a bed, one of three cramped into a small room of the family home. For seven long years, almost as much time as he had with his deceased family members, Bashir existed in a state of bliss. He was happy with Imran's family. As happy as he'd been with his own family. And he didn't see anything changing his mind.

He never saw the anxiety coming until it struck him. The rabid concern that he would lose everything and everyone was a bolt out of the blue. And he couldn't rid himself of it. All through the day it taunted him. He'd envision losing his new family to another freak accident. Each day that passed him, he kept watch for the calamity that would snatch his newfound happiness away. Never knowing what exactly would change his fortune to misfortune again, but he was certain the other shoe would drop eventually.

Only Imran had noticed the change in him. But no matter how he tried to get Bashir to open up, it didn't work. Finally, Bashir had done the only thing that had seemed sensible to him. He'd run away from the happiness first, before it got taken away from him. Literally.

Stowing away on an inflatable dinghy—one of many smugglers were using—Bashir squeezed in with dozens of scared but hopeful asylum seekers who were also looking to flee their lives in Somalia. The journey to Greece had been arduous and dangerous. It ended months later in an isolated and awful refugee camp on a rocky, forsaken Cretan islet. It wasn't the place for a runaway fourteen-year-old boy. Yet it had become his home for years. In a way his salvation too. He no longer had to worry about losing those he loved. After all, he'd walked away first. And without his risky travel and the camp he wouldn't be where he was now, blessed with richness and successes. He also might not even have gotten the chance to be Zaire's dad.

But Bashir *was* his father. And it was his single driving reason to make Zaire's life the antithesis of what his upbringing had been. Zaire deserved the childhood Bashir was robbed of when he lost his family. He would fight to his dying breath to give his son every joy and opportunity life could afford him. Just as he would ensure nothing harmed or distressed him. He owed that much and more to Imran. Bashir couldn't save his cousin, but he would do whatever he could for Zaire.

Which was why, if this was a prank or ploy, Bashir hoped his uninvited guest knew who she was up against.

And if it isn't?

If this woman had a message of import about his Zaire, he needed to hear it.

"Shall I see her delivered to the coast guard?"

Nadim mistook his ponderous silence for displeasure, and he was offering a reasonable solution. Just not the one he was leaning toward.

Bashir drummed his fingers atop the tablet and then flipped it back over again. He willed himself to stare deep into those fearsome eyes of this mysterious caller of his. No memory slotted into place. Her face was an enigma—literally shrouded by her shawl. The only connection was that she had been a nurse at the hospital where Zaire had been delivered. "Is she still on board?"

"She is."

Bashir tightened his fingers around the tablet, glowering at the image that would haunt him if he allowed it. And there were enough phantoms from his past to contend with. He didn't need to add one more ghost.

"Bring her to me."

It was the only way he'd solve the mystery and perhaps salvage the peace he'd almost achieved.

CHAPTER TWO

"NOT AGAIN…"

Yusra grumbled under her breath as she ripped the late rent notice off her apartment door. She heard a door unlatch down the hall and quickly stuffed the piece of offending paper in her floppy, well-worn purse before her neighbor stepped out into the hallway.

"Yusra, how are you?" Dembe paused in front of her, his smile as infectiously happy as always. He was a few years younger than her twenty-seven years, but that hadn't stopped her from noticing how finely built he was. Lean arms and toned legs squeezed into a polo shirt, tweed vest and jeans. She knew he hit the gym regularly between his long working hours at an international bank. He pushed his glasses up his nose and peered at her through them before flicking a look at her closed apartment door. Exactly where the notice had been affixed seconds ago. "Is AJ inside, or were you headed out?"

Dembe meant her son, Abdul Jabir.

"He's at day care today." She didn't add that she'd had to beg the day care owner again to overlook the late monthly payment Yusra owed her. It wouldn't be long before she'd have to find another arrangement for her son while she was working. But for today, she had a safe place for him to be cared for, and she'd have to be thankful for that.

One battle at a time.

Dembe beamed. "Oh, that's good. Let him know I'm happy to do that rematch later if he isn't too tired when he comes home." Dembe had been teaching her son to play football on weekends and whenever he had free time during the workweek. Yusra thought it was sweet of him, but she didn't want to monopolize his time.

"You don't have to—"

"I know, but I want to," he emphasized with a shrug and smile. "See, the little man has real moves on the field. A future Bwalya or Okocha."

The names meant nothing to her, but then she wasn't a super football fan like Dembe and her son.

"That's why I would hate him wasting that talent sitting around at home. So, I'll see you and AJ later." He waved to her and squeezed past, the narrow corridor forcing them closer together so that when he brushed her arm with his, he smiled and winked.

Yusra pressed cool hands to her inflamed

cheeks after he turned the corner toward the stairwell.

Her little crush on him was amusing. Nothing she sought to pursue, mostly because she was busy making ends meet, but also as she didn't want to ruin the friendship Dembe had fostered with her young son. Yusra's heart pattered at his thoughtfulness. Dembe didn't have to entertain a two-year-old—three in a few months—and yet he did, and he never seemed to heed her protests to the contrary.

If she had wanted to date anyone, Dembe would be a serious contender.

But she didn't.

And she owed it to the bad breakup with AJ's father, Guled. Though she didn't feel anything for him anymore, there had been a point in her life where Yusra had felt like she'd needed her ex-husband more than she needed air to breathe. She had loved Guled immensely and sacrificed plenty to keep him happy with her. He hadn't liked her working as an artist, so she'd packed up her tools and easel and sold them. Then when she'd switched to a career in graphic design and secured a job at a leading international marketing firm, Guled hadn't been satisfied with her commitment to long office hours and going on work-related trips with coworkers he didn't preapprove. Eventually he had told her to quit, and she'd caved and listened to him, letting go of a job she had liked. He hadn't wanted anyone else to get close to her. Nothing and no one else could matter but him. Not that those same rules applied to him.

No, he could go out and party all night long with his friends, while I sat home alone.

In all their years together, he hadn't ever bothered to invite her along for a night out. Almost as though he was embarrassed of her. Funny how it still stung to think about it. That was probably the worst part of their relationship for Yusra. Even after he'd pressured her into giving up on her art and then her job at the marketing firm, isolated her in their small apartment, gotten her pregnant, made promises that he would do right by her...she'd still wanted to see the good in him. The good in her love for him.

Of course he had then divorced her when he thought it too much of a bother to control her anymore. And it wasn't enough that he was leaving her, he hadn't wanted anything to do with their baby either. He'd refused to pay any child support or play any caregiving role, and he had told her parents as much once Yusra had called to inform them of the divorce.

It was perfectly normal that the implosion of her marriage to Guled had soured her on the idea of romance, except what she found in books, film and television.

At least between the pages of a book and on-screen she was safe from heartache.

The smile on her face vanished when she recalled the paper in her purse, the one she'd hidden away in panic. After pulling it out, she skimmed the short but succinct note from her landlord and sighed. It warned that she had all but a week to produce both last month and the current month's rents. Seven days and a few hundred American dollars to satisfy her landlord. What was she supposed to do in that short amount of time?

The panic started up again.

It coalesced into a fiery ball and fixed itself in her throat. She swallowed around the bilious heat ineffectually. As long as her bank account remained nearly drained, she wouldn't rid herself of the heartburn-inducing anxiety of providing a roof and shelter for her family. Her son was counting on her.

Yusra breathed deeply and whispered, "Calm down."

Packing the notice demanding rent and threatening eviction back in her purse, she then made sure to lock up and set off toward her office, praying that she would have more luck with her clients today. Her graphic design business might be operating out of the back room of a laundromat, but it was still serious work and she hoped luck was on her side and a steady source of revenue would flow in her direction. She needed it desperately.

As desperately as she needed shade when she stepped outdoors and the dry early summer heat clung to her like plastic wrap.

She waded through both the summery climate and the crowds, squeezed into an overcrowded bus and was dropped off onto the winding streets that led to her business. The laundromat was as busy as it could get during the day. Several mothers were juggling minding their young children and folding laundry, but there were also bored-looking students scrolling through their phones while waiting on their full cycle to finish. The laundromat owner monitored everything from behind the service desk with a phone pressed to her ear.

Yusra raised a hand in greeting and had hoped to pass through to the back unnoticed.

No such luck. The owner crooked a finger at her and briefly paused her lively chat to whoever was on the other end of the phone.

"Where's my rent?"

"I…" Yusra grappled for an excuse. She did a mental run of the ones she'd used before. "I'll have it soon," she finally said, settling on the vague truth.

The owner sucked her teeth and looked ready to tell her to pack up her office and clear out.

She wouldn't blame her if she did. She'd skipped out on two months' rent. The backlog of payments was beginning to overwhelm her almost as much as her business toeing the red in her books and her bank account dwindling faster than her nearly empty fridge. She had a growing child and she was awake all night from constant worry that one day she wouldn't be able to feed him. And what kind of mother would she be then?

The kind who shouldn't be a mom, she thought disparagingly of herself, almost as much as she denigrated the situation she didn't have full control of. It wasn't her fault entirely that her design services weren't in demand. But she knew she could hunt for other jobs. Plenty of unsavory ones that would still add some money to her pocket. They wouldn't make her happy the way designing on her computer did, but they would keep her son's belly full and give him a warm bed and a fluffy pillow to lay his head on at night.

The stress brought familiar pricks of tears to her eyes. Frustration sparked and crackled in her. She sucked in a deep, clarifying breath and was just about to stand her ground and plead her case when she watched the owner flick her eyes away to a point behind Yusra.

She turned and confronted a shocking sight. Five well-dressed men stood behind her, four of them with briefcases and one in a doctor's white coat over his fancy business suit.

The doctor one smiled directly at her. "Are you Ms. Yusra Amin?"

She frowned but nodded slowly, too tongue-tied to ask how he knew who she was and what he wanted.

"It's good we found you." The doctor held out his hand. "I'm the chief medical officer of Kampala City International Hospital."

Her eyebrows sprang up with her surprise. She hadn't visited the hospital since AJ's birth, but she knew they had her file, which *still* didn't explain how they had come to track her to her office out of the laundromat.

"How did you know to find me here?"

"We stopped by your apartment, and your landlord told us you conducted business in this building."

Yusra bit the inside of her cheek before she snapped that the landlord should have consulted her first. But she knew that the man had a grievance with her about her late rent payments and the eviction he persisted on threatening her with every time he saw her.

Nothing she could do about that now. She narrowed her eyes at all the men, memorizing their features and anything unique about them that stood out, in case they meant her harm. Not that she had a clue why she deserved it. Aside from late payments, she hadn't broken any laws or hung around any shady, suspect figures. Just Dembe, and he was her cute, generous-hearted neighbor.

Still, she gulped.

"May we speak with you in private?" The doctor smiled but the emotion felt forced rather than genuine.

"Sure," she said, possibly against her better judgement, and pointed out her office. "My office is over this way, if you'll follow me."

Only the doctor and one of the briefcase-carrying suits followed her. Good decision. Her tiny office wouldn't be able to hold more guests than that. She even had two seats for them across the small desk she'd wedged into the space. Squeezing around the scarred desk, she dropped into her chair and fanned out both her hands after they had gotten as comfortable as possible on the old spindly-legged wooden chairs.

"Now, what is this all about? And do I require a lawyer?" She laughed nervously at her joke. When they didn't join in, her heart sank into her stomach. Very weakly, and after a few thick swallows, she managed to say, "*Do* I need a lawyer present?"

Before either dour-faced man said anything, the closed door to her office boomed so loudly, the hinges heaved and squawked from the force.

What now? she fretted.

The pounding came again and both men looked at her expectantly. It was her office, and she ought to answer the door. Yusra slowly rose on her quaking legs and weakly called out permission for entry.

She hadn't finished speaking when the door opened in answer and a giant of a man revealed himself. Yusra couldn't believe her eyes. She was ashamed when she did a double take at first. He was just so…*big.* Tall. At least six-feet-nine or even taller. And he was thickly muscled too. His expensive-looking dress suit strained at his biceps and around trunk-like thighs. He had a wild long bushy beard to match those fierce eyebrows, and his black-as-night hair was on the longish side too and slicked back from his sculpted, hard-planed face. He was dark-skinned, yellowish brown, and that only made his dark eyes and dark facial hair that much more appealing.

But he was dressed finely in a three-piece blue-gray suit—arguably finer than the men sitting in her office.

Whoever this big man was, he took up space in more ways than just his physical presence. There was an unspoken authority that oozed off him and demanded all attention to him in a flash. He filled her doorway and had to stoop to get his head past the doorframe safely.

Soon as he entered, he passed a glance over the men before his sights zeroed on her.

She flinched…but not out of fear. Her body was responding to the electric current that inexplicably charged through her when their eyes collided.

"Yusra Amin." His voice was as mesmerizingly deep as he was large all over.

Also, unlike the other men, this newcomer spoke with confidence. And with that same confidence, he never took his eyes off her and addressed the men gruffly, "Nothing more will be said until Ms. Amin's lawyer joins this meeting."

Nothing had gone according to plan from the minute Bashir had discovered he'd arrived too late to intercept the bureaucratic goons from the hospital. Even if he had thought quickly on his feet and cleared them out of the cramped little room, it didn't change the fact that Yusra Amin looked ready to flee from him at any moment.

Her naturally round eyes narrowed at him from across the room. A tiny desk he could easily brush aside was the only thing separating him from her. But he didn't budge, studying her as warily as she was him.

Though she had more of a reason to suspect him. *He* had barged into her office, and not the other way around.

No matter. He expected some resistance on her part. What Bashir hadn't readied himself for was to be slightly frazzled when he saw her. This woman wasn't who he was expecting. She was attractive. Pretty in an understated way that could be polished into a quiet but powerful elegance. For that she'd have to be dressed in something other than a softly worn long-sleeved shirt and faded jeans. He would also have swapped the coarse dark blue shawl of her hijab for a material and color that complemented her rich brown skin better. And her long, graceful neck would look lovely adorned in the kind of gold that would make a sheikh's wife jealous.

Flickering his eyes up to her face, he frustratingly noted his attraction to her. But he wouldn't be deterred by any spontaneous feelings.

"We don't have much time."

"Who are you?"

Grateful that she spoke up, he realigned his thinking and answered her. "Introductions can happen later. What matters is that those men who were sitting here will be back soon." Once the hospital officials realized who he was and what was happening, they'd come knocking the way he had done. "It isn't long before we lose this window of opportunity to clear the air."

Yusra crossed her arms. "I would prefer the introductions happen now rather than later."

Bashir saw from her defensive posturing that he wouldn't get anywhere by pushing back against her. Time was a problem. She just didn't see that yet, as she wasn't working with the whole picture the way he was. And even though he had hoped to delay it by a little bit longer, he had no other option.

He pulled a sharp breath in through his nose. Then with a courage he hadn't yet fully subscribed to, he gave her what she'd asked for.

"My name is Bashir Warsame, and our sons were swapped at birth."

CHAPTER THREE

"DID YOU HEAR ME?" Because it looked like Yusra hadn't from Bashir's vantage point.

She stood eerily still, her arms still folded over her chest, her shirt's stretchy material curving tighter around her breasts—

He pulled a mental wall down between himself and where the rest of that thought had been leading him. Especially right then. Inopportune didn't begin to describe the sudden spike in his libido.

Growling low from an overwhelming sense of frustration, he snapped, "It's imperative that you listen to me."

"Why?" she whispered, but it carried loudly in the silence blanketing the shoebox of an office. "So you can spout off some more nonsense."

He scoffed in disbelief. "Nonsense?" Had she really just said that to him? He got that the whole switched-baby angle was ripped off the script of a melodrama, but he wasn't trying to fool her. This was his life now. And hers—whether she perceived him to be a liar or not.

But he supposed he could try to convince her again. He gnashed his teeth, frustrated with himself for noting the sweet scent of her perfume when she shifted closer to him.

"You should leave, before you wear out my patience."

"Ya Allah," he growled under his breath, *his* patience wearing out rapidly. With a quick calming breath sawing in and out of his flaring nostrils, he tried to reason with her one last time. "I understand it comes as a shock." He would know. Two days had hardly let his new reality sink in. He was still fighting against the riptide of doubt and hope that the baby-swap nightmare was just that, a nightmare that he left behind when he arose from bed. Only it wasn't.

From the moment the former nurse had walked into his office aboard his yacht, his life had changed irrevocably. Now all he could do was move forward and cope with it.

And he'd been doing just fine for a while. Bashir had bought the costly service of a private investigator and had finally tracked an address to Yusra. Sadly, the information had come to him an hour too late. Now he had the hospital breathing down his neck, vying to get to Yusra first, and possibly poisoning the waters for him to persuade her away from filing a lawsuit. At least one in the public court. He didn't want to imagine what that would do to Zaire to have their private world infiltrated by dangerously curious gossipmongers. Even though he was confident that no family court would simply sign off on Yusra taking his son from him, he was still cautious—smartly so.

"A couple of days ago, I had a visit from a former hospital employee. A nurse. She alleges that our sons were switched shortly after birth."

Shaking her head, her suspicion written all across her pretty face, Yusra said, "I don't know who you are, but that's a sick thing to say to anyone, let alone a mother."

"A sick thing, yes, but it's also the *truth*. If you give me a moment to explain, I would happily do so." He regarded his blue steel, blue-strapped watch and clenched his jaw until the pain there superseded the headache marching through his skull. "I never repeat myself, but I will stress once again that we are pressed for time."

"For someone who is trying to convince me, you're being awfully rude." She lowered her arms, began rummaging through her purse, and whipped out her phone. "It doesn't matter though. Whatever you're attempting to accomplish won't work. I won't call the police if you leave now and never show your face again."

"I've given you my name, you have seen my face and," he waved an arm out to gesture to the closed door at his back, "all those people out there have seen me come in here too. If I really wanted to do you any harm, wouldn't I have tried something already?"

What could he do to open her eyes to that fact?

Bashir recalled the conversation he'd had with Nadim before he had left his senior master to care for his yacht, staff, and Zaire.

"Why tell this Yusra anything at all?" Nadim had asked him. *"Simply if she tries to sue, we'll counter with a lawsuit of our own."*

He hadn't answered Nadim. Normally he wouldn't have thought twice and taken that very action against Yusra and whatever harm she could pose him. But this involved his son. His family. He had to tread carefully.

Admittedly, he'd been curious too. The son that Yusra had raised was his cousin, Imran's son. He wouldn't rest easy until he knew that the boy was being raised by a suitable caregiver. And he also had to know that Yusra wouldn't try to battle him for custodial rights to the child who was biologically hers. Zaire.

So he hadn't come spoiling for a fight with her.

That, and he knew any of this leaking to the press and public would stymie his business dealings and upend his private life. When he'd told her they didn't have much time, he hadn't only been concerned about the hospital board looking out for themselves.

This baby-swap fiasco had caught him at a bad time. Though the world might think him an idle billionaire, Bashir was far from free of scheduling burdens and the sleepless nights that came with shouldering the livelihoods of his expansive staff. He had a multinational company to run. Thousands employed at his many hotel locations. People with families and financial obligations who relied on his business to bring home the bread and butter. If he stopped, they suffered. On top of overseeing that his business endeavors ran smoothly from the comfort of his ocean-faring home, there was the matter of his nonprofit refugee organization, Project Halcyone.

The ground breaking for the organization's headquarters was well underway. Having funded most of it out of his own pocket, Bashir had expedited construction and expected it to wrap up in the coming few months. Just in time for the end of summer. Then he had plans to garner more funds from generous donors. Donors he anticipated wooing at a charity gala on the opening of Project Halcyone's main office.

Being a migrant himself once, he understood the momentous change this nonprofit could bring to fellow asylum seekers and runaways. He didn't like speaking about his origins. It always left his chest with a terrible pressure, yet he'd had to set those feelings of discomfort aside when an overzealous reporter at a leading European business journal came knocking. Declining the phone interview had been a thought he'd indulged but couldn't afford. Halcyone needed funding to keep its doors open. What better way to do that than by the free publicity a reputable journal could bring? Of course he had known to choose his words carefully. Not all free advertising was good marketing. Some unpalatable parts of his past as an undocumented immigrant teen would surely do more harm to his image and that of Project Halcyone.

It should have helped that he had interviewed with the reporter before. Only instead of the regular questions he'd expected to be asked, the interview had swerved into his past and remained there for most of the half-hour appointment. No matter what he'd tried, no excuse had been enough to end the interview. His family was brought up. As were his years in the refugee camp—though gratefully no mention about his brush with local Greek police when he'd been an angry, sullen teenager. Answering vaguely hadn't satisfied the overenthusiastic reporter. But he'd done his best, and still he had gotten off the call concerned that who he once was wasn't the only thing in danger of being revealed… Were the reporter to discover Yusra and the switched-at-birth drama with their sons, Bashir would have more trouble on his hands.

Trouble he didn't need.

For Project Halcyone to stand a chance, he required positive press and zero scandal around him as its founder. Bashir wouldn't allow anyone, not even a well-meaning mother like Yusra, to block him from making Halcyone a reality.

In a flash of inspiration, he grabbed one of the chairs that the hospital officials had vacated. Under his crushing bulk, the wobbly-legged old chair creaked and he might have blushed, but it was a scenario he was accustomed to experiencing—undersized furniture that could barely hold him in a world and environment that hadn't considered his comfort. But sacrifices had to be made in the face of extraordinary trouble.

Sacrifices that included balancing precariously on the thin legs of a too-small chair…

And looking Yusra Amin dead in the eyes before delivering the blow he prayed would have her see reason.

"Inshallah, my son will celebrate his third birthday on the first of September. And, if I'm not wrong, I believe he shares that in common with your son."

Quiet as a mouse now, Yusra's eyes widened and her alluring rosy-brown lips parted softly.

"Am I wrong?" he challenged.

She slowly shook her head and her grip on her phone trembled lightly. That was the instant he knew he had her.

* * *

My son. Your son.

The two phrases ran through her head in concentric circles. Like two suns in a binary system. Dancing around each other, until one tipped out of axis and collided into the other in a stellar explosion. An explosion that rocked her world, perhaps literally as the room began to tilt, spin and swim from her perspective.

Yusra squeezed her eyes shut.

A moment later she startled and opened her eyes at the touch on her shoulder. Big, warm and shockingly gentle given his impressive size and the gruffness with which he'd spoken to her.

Now, oddly, concern gleamed back at her in those starless dark pupils of his.

He'd called himself Bashir.

He bowed his head closer, astoundingly graceful even when he had to contort down to her level.

"If you're feeling dizzy, it helps to put your head between your legs."

She opened her mouth to tell him that it was his fault she suddenly felt sick to her stomach. But instead, she pushed away from him, turned her head and groped for the metal trash can under her desk. She clung to it until the immediate danger of sickness wore off and left her head feeling fuzzy and her mouth feeling absurdly dry.

"Water," she croaked.

As soon as she spoke, he left her in the office alone. She'd thought he abandoned her and almost laughed, wondering why she hadn't considered embarrassing herself earlier by retching out her breakfast to get him to leave her alone. If she weren't so weak, she'd have celebrated her victory over him. But she conserved her strength. Wiping her mouth, she set down the trash bin, and laid her forehead down on her arms atop her desk.

It wasn't long before she raised her head at the sound of the door clicking open once more.

"Water," said her hulking interrogator, his tone as gravelly as ever.

Annoyed that he helped her, Yusra accepted the water bottle and drank greedily from it. The fog around her mind cleared a bit, but the dryness remained in her mouth, and the weakness anchoring her bones and muscles still persisted as well.

"Food?" he said, reading her thoughts.

She flitted through her purse, this time determined to be her own hero, and unwrapped the straw of an orange juice box. It was a quick-fire way of knowing she wouldn't be knocked out by low blood sugar. As it was, she was reeling from what he had told her.

What she now tried and failed to pretend wasn't happening—which was impossible because it *had* happened.

My son. Your son.

Your son. My son.

She gave her head a jerk to clear her mind; little help it did. The words were seared in her brain. The truth almost too hard to bear.

"I was shocked too at first."

She sucked hard at her straw and flashed a quick, narrowed gaze at him, not ready to trust him enough with her feelings. She barely wrapped her mind around what he had said, but somehow, despite the clanging alarm for her to remain suspicious and cautious and argumentative—she *knew* that he was telling the truth. How else would he know her son's birthday?

It didn't stop her from blurting, "How do I know you're not some stalker who did your research?" Her voice was soft but accusatory. Anger laced her question too. Because she had nowhere else to direct the toxic and burdensome emotion. Unfortunately for him, he was the only suitable target in the room.

Though he didn't appear ruffled by it. He sat across from her again. Sitting up as tall and confidently as he was on his feet, he cocked his head and interlocked his hands between his legs.

"I could be a stalker, yes. But if I wanted to hunt you, Yusra, you *would* know."

"Oh, would I?" She rolled her eyes but froze when she saw his bushy black eyebrows snap down. When his lips moved, his smooth, deep voice pushed frantically at a primal button in her. She locked her legs together against the responsive heat from her feminine core.

"Yes, you would," he rasped darkly.

Under the weight of her hijab, her scalp prickled more, sweat lining her brow where her headscarf concealed her hairline. Even with the extra layers, there was this unsettling sense of exposure being around him brought out in her. More now that she noticed he was startlingly good-looking in a certain light. His face was all angles, brutally sharp cheekbones, a jawline that was strongly square, and a nose that hooked at the bridge before widening at the base. Dark brown lips were wide and pillowy and took up enough attention without his long, curly beard circling them. Funny thing being that his mouth was the only part of him that appeared soft, *and* he hadn't stopped frowning since he entered her office the first time.

Yusra blushed the more she took in of him. Her cheeks toasty hot by the time her eyes zipped up to meet his gaze.

The instant she did, her feverish skin began to cool. It happened suddenly. Ice-cold water poured over her head and froze the swift heated response to Bashir.

What am I thinking?

He had given her life-changing news, and instead of worrying about the safety of her family—

about *protecting* her son, she was drooling over a man. Disgust rose up through her, curdling hot and nauseating. What kind of mother was she?

"What did you mean earlier?" she asked, hearing the fear in her voice and unable to do anything to plug its source. "How were our children... How could that even happen?"

"Our sons were accidentally swapped by an overworked, underpaid NICU nurse. The mistake was overlooked for years, and she'd sought to fix the problem on her own. She lost her job because of the error."

"That's awful." Yusra forgot she had the juice box in her hands until she squeezed the carton so hard that the juice oozed out onto her hands. She tugged napkins out of her purse, ignoring the fist crushing her heart when she had to move aside a pack of her son's favorite snack bars to get to the tissues.

But according to Bashir, AJ wasn't really hers. For nearly three years she'd raised him thinking he was her flesh and blood. The only good that had come out of his hopeless, heartless father.

No! It didn't matter what anyone had done in the past. AJ *was* hers!

"Let's say all of this is true, and our children were swapped, what are you planning to do?"

"Right now, those men out there are hoping to

sweep this mess under the rug. They'll offer you money. Buy your silence."

"And you? Will you do the same?" Her belly quivered from the overload of nerves. There was a real possibility she'd heave the orange juice she'd drunk.

Big shoulders rising and falling subtly with the softest of sighs, he told her, "I won't lie to you and say I wasn't curious about the child."

He meant her son.

Her stomach hollowed. Weakly, she protested, "You can't take him. He's mine."

"And my son is mine." He scowled. "Do you think that's what I want? To steal your child? I won't delude myself to thinking that you trust me. I'd be a hypocrite if I expected that."

His meaning was clear. He didn't trust her either.

Bashir stared hard at her. "The truth is, my curiosity doesn't overpower my desire to protect my own child."

It struck her right then that he probably wanted to make this go away just as much as she did.

Yusra knew what it meant. She'd have to relinquish her biological tie to his son. She didn't even know the other child's name, but she worried if she heard it, she wouldn't be able to walk away. If she wanted this to go away, she had to turn her back on what could have been and recall that her present life had been perfectly happy before this bombshell went off in her office.

Okay! Truthfully, she could do with a bit more money. But that was because she was constantly anxious that she wouldn't be able to keep a roof over their heads or give her son everything in life that he deserved.

"We could walk away from this, right here and now," he intoned. "No costly legal battle needed."

Could she do it? Could she walk away knowing that she had another child out there?

Her heart fluttered and her insides swooped.

There must have been some sign of indecisiveness on her face that prompted Bashir into saying, "I have a suggestion."

She tensed but didn't stop him from continuing. "Think on it."

"And then what?" Yusra challenged with a frown, her heart thudding and her leg bouncing from her nerves. She didn't think there was a chance that he'd just leave and never bother her again. She wasn't even *certain* she wanted him walking away like this, given everything that had happened. Because she still had questions she wanted answered.

Bashir rose to his feet, his tall, heavily built frame pulling up gracefully from the small chair he somehow managed not to break. He glanced cursorily at the walls of her office, presumably at the sketches and paintings she'd framed and hung. She had used a variety of mediums. Charcoal, watercolors, oil and even newsprint to create her art. These pieces were the only ones she hadn't gotten rid of and managed to hide from her controlling ex-husband. She had hung them to remember what she had gotten through. How she had survived a disastrous divorce and thrived as a single mother. But also to recall she'd had a passion once.

"You're an artist?"

"Graphic designer, actually." Small talk wasn't what she wanted though. Thankfully he was of the same mindset.

"You don't have to decide at the moment."

She raised a brow, arguing, "What happened to having little time?" She slung his words back at him.

Perfectly timed, a rapping sounded at the door to her office. It had to be the hospital personnel that Bashir had ushered out earlier.

Unheeding of the noise behind him, he pulled his analyzing gaze from her art and on to her. "Being pressed for time is always a factor in big, life-altering decisions."

The impatient knocking started up again. *Rat-tat-tat*.

"However, I *would* suggest calling a lawyer," Bashir continued calmly. "It'll help keep the hospital from imposing what's best for them on to you. And here's my card." She allowed him to place it on her desk without protest even though she wasn't sure she would contact him.

"Once you've processed this, call or email me."

"What if I don't?" Yusra kept him from leaving. A minute ago, she would have been relieved to see him exit her office. But now she was confused about everything. Including what she wanted, or what the best recourse was for her.

He looked back at her over his broad shoulder, his face expressionless but his eyes overly compelling and a danger to her rabbiting heart.

"You will," he impressed on her. He said it so self-assuredly that it bordered on smug confidence.

And yet, she didn't have the words to knock his ego down a peg or hold him back from walking out of her office and leaving her to process everything that had gone down.

CHAPTER FOUR

DESPITE HER RESERVATIONS about Bashir, Yusra still took his advice and refused to speak to the hospital personnel who wanted to buy her silence. And she called a lawyer. Her neighbor Dembe assisted her there. Luckily his older brother worked in the legal field and got in touch with a colleague who specialized in family law.

Everything happened so fast.

Within a few hours of learning from Bashir that their sons had been swapped at birth, Yusra heard back from the lawyer, who had then advised her to sit on the nondisclosure agreement the hospital had left with her and agreed to legally represent her pro bono.

She hadn't spoken to Bashir again, but their lawyers were doing the talking for them. From what she understood, after four days of deliberation, Bashir and his legal team had returned with an astoundingly generous offer. So generous, she questioned its veracity until she read the details for herself and had her lawyer break down any legalese. Bashir was offering monetary compensation in the form of a trust fund for her son, AJ. The extra zeroes were what had her eyes bugging. She'd have to sign a nondisclosure, of course. It would bar her from ever speaking of the baby-swap incident. Which meant she would be giving up any chance at meeting her biological son—the child who Bashir was raising.

I still don't even know the child's name...

This wasn't a decision she could make lightly. There were repercussions and lifelong regrets to consider. Could she truly walk away now that she knew she had another child connected to her out there?

Maybe that was why she had asked to see Bashir. Speak to him once more.

He agreed to meet with her on his yacht, requesting that they leave their lawyers behind.

She reluctantly accepted, but secretly worried whether he had the upper hand. They would be on his turf, not hers. It was hardly fair, yet she didn't see what choice she had, and especially when she felt this conversation would help her determine what choice was best.

Yusra didn't know what to expect after assenting to both of his stipulations on their meeting grounds.

But it wasn't a luxury sedan picking her up

from her shabby apartment in her equally grungy neighborhood. The car ferried them through the congested traffic of Kampala to Entebbe International Airport where a private plane in a well-guarded hangar awaited their arrival. By that point she questioned her decision, but it was too late to back out, as her son reminded her.

Bringing AJ along had been instinctual. She hadn't wanted to leave him behind. Needed the comfort of his presence. Lately more than ever. Deep down she couldn't shake this unease that he could be taken from her. Irrational, perhaps. But considering the baby swap, was it such a stretch for her to be overly protective? So long as he was in her sight, she couldn't lose him.

And unlike her, AJ liked the idea of them boarding a plane.

She'd already promised him a tour of Bashir's boat—not that she'd asked Bashir himself. That was the least of her problems though.

The flight lasted a little less than two hours before the pilot announced they'd reached the international airport in Mombasa, Kenya. Another sleek sedan whisked them from the airport to what Yusra hoped was their final destination. Bashir's ship.

They were traveling alongside the ocean. Deep blue waters endlessly rippling into the sun-blurred horizon. She rested her forehead on the cool glass of the car window and gazed at the large body of water, nostalgia flooding into her instantly. It reminded her of home and just how close she was to Somalia since she'd left her country to study and work in Uganda. When she'd lived with her parents and siblings, the beach and ocean were a short walking distance from her family home. She had spent many an evening with family members and friends just lounging in the sands and playing in the water. She hadn't realized just how much she missed it…

Until now, she thought sadly.

Her sadness faded when her ocean view was cut off by a large ship. She knew, straightaway, that it belonged to Bashir. Nothing that big could be cheap. Only a billionaire could afford the gleaming white monstrosity floating in the ocean. She'd met one such billionaire recently.

And she wasn't the only one who noticed the change in scenery. Beside her, AJ wriggled against his seat belt and gripped her hand tighter. "Look, Mama! Boat!"

"I see it, sweetheart," she said, her heart pumping faster.

Her son's excitement was contagious. It had to be. This giddy anticipation bubbling in her was a typical reaction to new experiences. The journey via a luxury car and private jet. Seeing the Indian Ocean again after so many years. Was it any wonder that her and AJ were overwhelmed? Visiting a boat was a first for them both—and Bashir's ship was massive.

The superyacht awaiting them seemed twice as large when she stepped out of the car with AJ balanced on her hip.

"Big boat!" AJ chirped at her and pointed to it. As though she could miss it.

She saw the big boat perfectly. But it was the big man waiting at the base of the walkway onto the giant yacht that had her body going rigid, her mouth dry and her belly all atwitter. That butter-flies-in-her-tummy reaction that no man had elic-ited from her since her divorce was alive and well and flapping innumerable tiny wings all through her, and for Bashir of all people. Not even her crush on her cute and sweet neighbor Dembe had gotten that kind of biochemical fireworks. Yusra didn't know what it meant that Bashir had pro-voked the response in her. Only that she shouldn't follow the dangerous lure of the attraction.

Bashir wasn't alone. Though flanked by two other men, both males impressively towering in height and brawny in muscle, he still stood out as the largest and strongest among them.

"Yusra." He acknowledged her with a curt nod and an intense gaze.

"Bashir," she replied.

Feeling the press of eyes all around them, and

the tight grip of AJ's fingers digging into her arm, she was reminded that they weren't here for a pleasure trip. She climbed the walkway, acutely aware of Bashir following her onto his ship. AJ wiggled in her arms, quietly asking to be let down. After gently setting him onto the teak flooring of the deck, she clutched his tiny hand and looked around at the unbelievable view from atop Bashir's tall and expansive yacht. She didn't have much time to take in her fill of the sights and sounds before he engaged her in conversation.

"Is this…?" It was strange to see hesitance flit across his stern face. The first time she believed he'd shown an expression that wasn't powerfully confident in the short while she'd known him.

"My son," she told him and completed his thought.

He made a two-finger motion to one of the men behind him. "It appears we had the same idea," he said with a snort, his message enigmatic until she saw what he meant.

A slightly older woman walked up to them. She had her dark brown hair scraped back into an austere braid and wore a plain long-sleeved white shirt and blue jeans. And she wasn't alone. She carried a young boy in her arms. A boy who had Yusra's dark reddish-brown coloring and curly black hair.

Without needing to confirm it, her eyes watered and she knew who he was.

Bashir's son.

Now she understood what he had said about their thinking alike.

She'd brought AJ along on the fly, convinced she was worried to let him out of her sight in case she lost him. But now she knew that wasn't the full truth. Because now she suspected it was for the same reason that Bashir had sent for his son. He wanted her to meet the boy.

And it seemed she wanted the same for him and AJ.

Bashir saw surprise blossom over Yusra's face. It started with her dark brown eyes rounding and her breath audibly catching. He suddenly and fiercely, to the marrow of his bones, wished she were gazing at him. But he wasn't the reason she was so taken aback.

Her eyes glued on to his son, she breathily asked, "What's his name?"

"Zaire." He'd chosen the name for his son as Tara and Imran had both died before doing the honor. Given how his beginning was tragic, Bashir had picked an empowering name that was indicative of Zaire's more fortunate future. "It means river that swallows all rivers." He didn't know why he was telling her that. Just like he didn't know why it mattered when she didn't laugh him off.

Rather than laugh, she blinked suspiciously several times and murmured, "It's a good name."

Without Bashir needing to ask, she stroked the wispy curls of the boy stuck fast to her leg and introduced him.

"This is Abdul Jabir. AJ for short."

"A strong name too," he told her.

The boy gaped up at him, the toy boat clutched in one small fist and holding his mother with the other hand. Meanwhile Zaire clung shyly to Alcina when she attempted to approach them more closely. Neither child seemed ready to meet new faces.

Bashir had anticipated this reaction. Prepared for it. The children weren't the only ones who seemed uncomfortable. He read a similar hesitance from Yusra. There was a rigidity to her posture. Her shoulders were drawn up and her eyes warily flitted over his face, the meaning in her actions clear to him. She wasn't sure whether she could trust him. And she had every right to her suspicions. He ticked off all the reasons. She was on his ship. She knew he had more money than she did. Certainly more legal power and sway. From her perspective, it wasn't a leap for her to be wondering if she was at his mercy.

The truth? She had something he wanted that

weighed far more than all his wealth and the power that came with it. Something he couldn't force from her. Glancing down at her son, and watching the boy shy away from him behind his mother again, Bashir felt his heart give a short, sharp lurch. A forlornness settled over him. This was Imran's son. To think that he might not ever have met him if that former nurse hadn't told him about the accidental baby swap. Not that he regretted having Zaire. Not for one second. He would trade anything to keep his son, but a new sensation muscled its way to the front of his mind.

Greed.

He wanted both boys. But he also wasn't willing to rob AJ from his mother. And Yusra didn't deserve that. From what he learned of his private investigation on her, she was poor, not a bad caregiver. In fact, she was the opposite. Worked hard to provide for herself and her child even when her business was slow and her income was scarce. It was obvious she'd do anything for AJ. He wouldn't break up their family just to satisfy this need to have the best of both worlds.

Grinding his teeth together at the conundrum facing him, he turned his thoughts to a problem he could solve. The awkward silence that had descended on them.

"I'll take him from here." Thanking Alcina

and dismissing her, he plucked Zaire from his nanny's arms. His son gripped him tightly but snuck peeks at their visitors. Fear clashing with curiosity. Neither one winning yet. It was a good enough cue for them to move on.

"I know we're meeting under serious circumstances, but I hoped I could interest you in a tour of the ship first. If that's all right with you?" He would give her every chance to back out. Prove to her that she wasn't as powerless as she might believe herself to be.

Yusra pulled her son up into her arms. Then with a jut of her chin, she informed him, "AJ wanted a tour anyways."

He couldn't have asked for a better response. "I'll have to aim to please then."

"But we will talk after, yes?"

"Of course, that's a given," he promised before leading the way through his ship.

As they traversed from stern to starboard to bow and port, he pointed out the amenities. Because that was what a person did on a tour of their home, flex all that his wealth could afford him. A sports court and golf tee, an infinity pool with a rock waterfall, the top-class wellness center he rarely used but probably should, one of two private cinemas—this one outdoors, an indoor garden and the helicopter deck. He had merely scratched the surface, but Zaire was growing

restless in his arms, and it appeared that Yusra
wasn't having it better than him with AJ. Fidg-
ety toddlers spelled trouble, so he changed tack
and ended their tour abruptly by heading to their
final stop. Zaire's playroom.

Yusra's first reaction was a breathy gasp. Then
she asked, "How is this even possible?" Awe
pulsed through her voice.

Bashir tried to see it the way she would. A
whole playground on a ship. His money was seriously talking now.

AJ wriggled down from Yusra, and though he
clutched his mother's hand, he toddled forward
with her. Equally eager to explore, Zaire jabbed
a finger at the swings and whined until Bashir
carried him to one of two full bucket seats on the
swing set of the sprawling play area.

Whatever shyness and fear had plagued both
boys thawed now that the prospect of play was
in front of them. Within minutes, AJ and Zaire
were squealing with laughter. Yusra was helping
AJ navigate the climbing structure, and Bashir
pulled Zaire from the swings when he'd gotten
bored and took him over to the remarkably colorful playhouse. Before long that turned into him
waiting on his son to climb out of a crawl tube
and trailing after him to where Yusra and AJ had
been playing on the climbing structure. Bashir
didn't know when he'd shed his suit jacket and

tie, or when he had rolled up his sleeves and un-
buttoned his collar. But it was less restrictive
chasing after his son without them on.

Zaire squeezed onto his lap and they slid down
the spiral slide together. But after a couple of
times doing this, his son stopped and sat on one
of the steps of the climbing structure to watch
Yusra rock AJ on a boat-shaped spring rider. AJ
rocked faster with her help and smiled toothily
up at his mother.

Zaire slowly moved from the climbing structure over to where they were, and he stooped to
pick up the toy boat that AJ had set aside temporarily in lieu of playing. By this point Yusra
noticed him and stopped what she was doing.

Intrigued, Bashir watched the interaction close
by. If Zaire needed him, he'd step in, but right
now his son seemed comfortable approaching
the newcomers.

Zaire held the toy up to Yusra.

She crouched smilingly to his level and ac-
cepted it on AJ's behalf. "Thank you, Zaire."
Casting a quick look back at her son, she asked,
"Would you like a turn to ride too?"

His son nodded timidly.

"What do we say when we ask for something
nicely?" Bashir asked his son.

Looking between them, Zaire then said, "Please."
Although it came out more like *puh-weeze*, it was

still enough for Yusra to smile so fully and with this glowing radiance that even his heart quickened at the sight of it.

Zaire was totally won over once Yusra pulled AJ off the spring rider and placed his son on the toy.

AJ didn't cry. Overly mature for his age, he stepped back with his toy boat grasped in his small hands. Bashir still hadn't acclimated to seeing him as Imran and Tara's son.

"I like your ship, little man."

"Boat," he said.

Bashir smirked at the correction, but agreed, "Boat."

Looking at the portrait they made, almost like they were one big happy and *normal* family, he realized this would be difficult.

It's going to be harder than I imagined or hoped it would be.

As though hearing his thought, Yusra flicked a look back at him. Her open expression echoed what he felt, and he sensed she'd agree that no part of this decision they'd have to make would be easy or painless.

Getting Yusra to himself took far longer than Bashir believed it would.

Eventually though both AJ and Zaire had gone down for their naps following an afternoon of play. They hadn't fussed either. Just exhausted themselves asleep soon as they were in bed. Bashir walked quietly for the exit, sensing Yusra behind him. He paused when she lingered at the door into the bedroom. Bashir knew what she had to be feeling because he felt it too. Looking over her head at their boys tugged at his heartstrings fiercely. They had bonded quickly enough, as though it was all second nature to them.

He wished it could be as easy between him and Yusra. Particularly with the direction his thoughts had angled after watching their sons interact positively.

Leaving the boys to nap, he guided his special guest to a salon, the largest of three on the yacht. The living space garnered the same reaction from her as Zaire's playroom had.

Her breath hitched and she stood still upon entering the room. "I don't know why I'm surprised it's so beautiful."

Bashir hid his smile with the excuse to hydrate them.

Pulling out two crystal-encrusted bottles from his mini fridge, he then pried the lids off with a bottle opener and walked over to where she was standing before one of many windows offering a postcard-perfect view of the ocean. She accepted the bottle with a tentative expression touching her brows, and her fingertips tracing the sparkling crystals lining the top and bottom of the bottle label.

"It's water," he explained, realizing he probably should have led with that.

"Should I bother asking why your water's pretty too?"

He did laugh now. A short-lived chuckle that grated at his throat and reminded him of how long it had been since he'd laughed. Long enough to feel embarrassed at the abrupt show of emotion.

Yusra seemed to recognize his faltering too. Her eyes rounder, dark pupils contracting as streams of sunlight brightened the salon. But what arrested him most was her bottom lip caught between her teeth. The smooth pink flesh tortured by her unease. Or maybe it was worry? He wouldn't know. Just as he didn't understand why she had such an effect on him. Only that she did, and it should concern him. Yet it didn't.

Staring at her for longer than could be deemed polite, he sipped his ice-cool water as an excuse to quench his sudden thirst and a chance to re-center his composure. Because what Bashir had to tell her next would take all of his focus and power of persuasion.

She drank slowly from the bottle too, licking her lips of any stray droplets and murmuring, "It tastes expensive."

Smiling tensely, he nodded, his mind already a few paces ahead.

"The boys seemed to love playing together," Bashir observed. "Zaire isn't used to having playmates, so I'll confess I was worried about how well he would share. But AJ seemed like he was used to it."

"He attends day care. Sometimes." Her voice pitched at the end, hinting that there was more to her statement. She didn't hold him in suspense for too long. "Childcare can be costly."

"I imagine it is. Especially when you want the best care for your little one."

She clasped the bottle with both her hands, her gaze avoidant now. "We aren't here to discuss that though, are we?"

"No, we aren't," he agreed, sensing that she needed truth more than anything, but also establishing as much rapport as he could squeeze into this moment. He needed her trusting him when he asked her what he had in mind. "Before we get to that, may I ask why you wanted to meet again?"

When he'd visited her in her office, he had given her his business card with little expectation. Especially once he'd had his lawyers send the offer of monetary compensation to her along with a nondisclosure to stop her from ever speaking publicly about the baby swap. Since Bashir clarified that the money would be held in trust for AJ until he came of age, he didn't think he'd hear back from Yusra. It had been a generous amount. But to him, it was a paltry fraction of what he owed Imran. Remorse throttled him whenever he thought of his cousin. Of the years he'd wasted not keeping in more regular touch with him. Now he was doing the same thing to his remaining family members. Imran's parents and siblings had tried reaching out before and after Imran's death, and Bashir had frozen them all out. If anything, losing Imran had reminded him that loss and death were unavoidable, and that caring and loving would only intensify the sense of loss and power of death that much more.

If he were being brutally honest with himself, he had wanted Yusra to take the money and vanish. It would have been easier on him. Instead, she'd called. Asked to meet. And he hadn't been able to deny her.

"I wanted to thank you. I wasn't expecting money." She bit her lip, walked to the glass sled coffee table and set down her bottle of water. "But I have to say, I won't accept the money if it's to pay me off."

"It isn't. Although I can appreciate why you might think it is." He couldn't tell her about Imran, and why he felt duty-bound to provide anything he could to AJ. Not yet. Maybe not ever, depending on how their conversation panned out. "To be clear, the money is exclusive of the non-disclosure."

He placed his bottle of water next to hers on the coffee table before dropping onto the leather sofa facing the incredible vista of the ocean. Shadowing him, Yusra grabbed the armchair diagonal to his position. This way they could face each other more comfortably.

Comfortable is a stretch...

Apprehension sucked the air out of the room.

Bashir believed taking this slowly would ease the pressure off him and give Yusra time to adjust, but the longer he held out, the worse his nerves jangled. He'd done enough tiptoeing around her. The more this continued, the less control he would have by the end.

"You could have thanked me over the phone," he remarked. "And why bring AJ?"

"I didn't want to leave him alone." The wrinkle between her fine eyebrows became more pronounced. "Besides, I could ask you the same thing. I hadn't expected to meet Zaire."

"I wanted to give him the chance to meet his birth mother. In case he never had the opportunity again."

Yusra shifted in her armchair, signaling her rising discomfort, and her hands closed into small fists atop her knees as though she was fighting her restlessness. Her lost hope. Bashir grazed his eyes over her. She had dressed modestly again, but her beauty wasn't muted. Disarmed by his attraction to her, he lowered his defenses.

"Recall that back in your office I asked you whether you could walk away. Now that you've had time to think on it, could you?"

"It would be harder now that I've met Zaire," she said.

"I feel the same about AJ."

She dipped her chin and smiled morosely. Even if he hadn't just heard her hesitation to part ways forever, he'd have seen enough by looking at her. She didn't want to walk away. But she was accepting the fact that she'd have to leave soon, and for good, once she signed off on the NDA to bury the baby swap. And naturally she mourned it.

As he should too. And he might have if he weren't clinging on to one last shred of hope.

"What if this visit didn't end?" he asked.

"What do you mean?"

He'd been thinking this over ever since he had seen AJ and Zaire together, in one room, playing carefree and cooperatively. Also whenever Zaire had approached Yusra and asked her to help push him on a swing or rock him on the spring rider toy. She hadn't treated his son any differently from her own. Except he'd caught a few long-ing glances from her toward Zaire, her mater-nal love unhidden and shining in her eyes. And why shouldn't she feel that way? He was her son.

Just as AJ was his family.

Seeing her apprehension staring back at him, he told her the plan he'd been ruminating on for the past hour. The plan he now believed truly had legs.

"What if AJ and Zaire could be in both our lives?"

"How?" she blurted. And just like that, her agitation wiped clear once he presented a solu-tion to their shared problem.

"Fair warning, it's unorthodox. But it will re-lieve us from having to choose to walk away."

"Tell me." An unspoken resolve caught fire in her coal-dark eyes, added a richer red to her deep brown skin and straightened her backbone. And before she opened her mouth, he knew she was willing to hear his wild idea.

Only it sounded even more outrageous when he spoke it.

"Marriage. If we were to marry, then the chil-dren could stay with us both, and having to walk away would no longer be a problem."

CHAPTER FIVE

"MARRIAGE?" YUSRA HEARD herself repeating slowly, enunciating the few syllables, and all while feeling foolish. Because surely, she'd heard him incorrectly.

Bashir couldn't have just asked to marry her.

It was more likely that she had allowed her hope to get the best of her. She didn't want to leave Zaire behind, and like her, Bashir hadn't wanted to let go of AJ. Naturally then, for one brilliant, buoyant second, she had thought he had found a way to fix this.

But Yusra's fleeting hope passed as quickly as it arose.

And she might have remained convinced she'd heard wrong if Bashir didn't speak up.

"Yusra. I'm very seriously proposing this."

"This can't be for real," she whispered as a wave of dizziness swamped her. She was glad she was seated when Bashir had turned her world upside down. Possibly as much as the baby swap had. Weakly, she protested, "It has to be a joke… Right?"

She would even be willing to forgive him if it was, as cruel as it would be.

"Marriage is serious. It's a lifelong commitment." Yusra felt like a hypocrite once she said it. Her marriage hadn't lasted. It also hadn't been full of love and support and reciprocity. And the experience soured the possibility of a second-chance romance for her. Still, it didn't mean she held any less value for the long-standing institution.

His frown was immediate and tinged with annoyance.

"I wouldn't joke about anything that required the level of trust a marriage demands. I've given this plenty of thought. I wouldn't have proposed it if I hadn't." He then set his jaw firmly, the veins along his temples more pronounced, his brows two furry lines of severity. "Marriage would allow us to live together with the children. It would also present a united front to the hospital. They want to fix their error, and they've already contacted me about having us swap our children and righting the wrong."

Yusra knew about the hospital's request, as they'd made it to her lawyer. It was why she'd been scared of losing AJ one way or another. That fear retriggered her anxiety, and she curled her hands into fists, her nails carving into the fleshy pads of her palms. "All right, but what made you decide this was the only way? We could co-parent without the ties of marriage."

"It might not seem like it, but I'm traditional," he countered.

"But marriage is complicated. There are things couples discuss and discover even before they consider such an important oath." Even as she spoke, Yusra knew not even a willingness to openly communicate could prevent a marriage from falling apart. She should be happy that Bashir wasn't asking love from her too.

"Then we'll talk and negotiate terms, and outline and sign off on them. I believe it's possible. However, if you're not on board…" He trailed off, with the clear intention that he didn't plan on forcing her into anything she didn't want a part of.

It lent her a modicum of comfort. Though not enough to win her over on to his idea yet.

"I'll have to think this through."

Bashir had given her time to muddle a decision once before, so she wasn't expecting him to nod albeit with a reluctant scowl.

"That's fine, but you'll have to think fast. This problem of ours is better solved sooner. One way or another."

Yusra sensed there was more to his urgency

that had to do with motives outside just wanting to spend limitless time with both their boys. And yet she agreed with him that the baby swap had shaken their lives, and nothing would begin to feel right again until they were unified on a decision.

That had been two days ago. Once she'd left the yacht and been returned to her tiny apartment, she'd given his suggestion plenty of thought, and after a grueling forty-eight hours, had come to a decision.

She would agree to marriage.

Yusra had thought this over long and hard. Sleep hadn't come easily to her the last two days. Every time she closed her eyes, she pictured Bashir's hard gaze, dark beard and his unsmiling but tempting mouth.

And during the day she couldn't help looking at AJ and wondering what Zaire was doing. She had her son around her more often now that he'd been removed from day care due to her inability to maintain his tuition. Which meant that she'd had no choice but to work from home or bring him along to client meetings in her small office out of the laundromat. It hadn't been an ideal arrangement, and though it had worked for now, she was aware it couldn't last forever. Mostly because AJ missed his friends and teachers in day care, and when he wasn't talking about that, he pelted her with questions about Bashir and Zaire. When were they going back to visit Bashir's big boat? When could he play again with Zaire's adorable albino rabbit, Puzzles? When was Zaire going to come and visit their home like they had visited his?

Yusra hadn't factored in the two toddlers bonding as fast as they had. She'd only considered her and Bashir's feelings on the matter. But clearly the boys missed each other, and Bashir's proposal of marriage did ensure that they'd live together like a family. It was starting to look less and less like an absurd idea after all...

And she wasn't entirely ignoring the fact that he was still offering to help with money. Just before she'd left his yacht, he had assured her that AJ's trust fund would remain, regardless of her decision on the marriage proposal. Having that nest egg for AJ lightened a load she didn't even know she had been shouldering. Knowing that Bashir cared for AJ as much as he did Zaire warmed her more to his plan for them to be family.

During the day it all seemed so logical and clear...

But at night, when she was alone with her traitorous dreams about Bashir's handsome face and big, strong body drifting closer to her, she succumbed to doubts as quickly as she did to temptation. She always woke up in the sanctuary of her bed, far, far from Bashir, but it didn't shift her unease about what life would be like actually living with him. Being near him a lot more. Possibly even sharing a bed with him.

No, that doesn't have to happen. That's where I'll draw the line.

At least that was what she promised she would do when she saw him next. And now that the moment had come, she was nervous and nowhere near as confident in discussing the possibility of intimacy between them.

Bashir sat across from her, his legal team filling his half of the conference table, while her lone lawyer sat next to her. Just the two of them against a whole army, and the billionaire general who led the charge. They had barely been seated when she agreed to his marriage proposal. All eyes on her, she fought against the knee-weakening embarrassment scoring her cheeks and fluttering through her stomach.

"Did you hear me?" she asked after Bashir showed no outward reaction to what she'd said.

"Just fine," he replied.

Why was he acting so strangely? His tone flat, and his expression without affect—although she'd grown used to seeing him like that. Bashir didn't express too much emotion since she had met him. But it would have been nice to have some reaction from him. Wasn't he thrilled that she was consenting to his wild proposal? Some fanfare from him would have been encouraging.

Disappointed, Yusra felt a spike in her anxiety again as a new thought struck her.

What if he's changed his mind?

Considering it had taken working up all her nerve to do this, she wouldn't be happy with him. Her choice went against both her lawyer's and Dembe's advice to reconsider Bashir's unconventional solution to their swapped-babies issue. Her neighbor had been the only other person who had known, and that was because she felt she owed him, considering he'd helped secure her a lawyer in the first place.

It was for the best that the less people knew in her life, the better. *For now.* She'd only drag her family into this when she was certain.

And if Bashir had changed his mind after all, she didn't want one more person knowing that she'd been rejected.

Yusra quelled the instinct to fidget in her seat. The ticking of the wall clock wasn't helping calm her. It felt like a countdown to a timer.

Or a bomb, she thought grimly.

Flicking a glance at the clock, she wondered whether AJ was having fun with Dembe. Her kindly neighbor had volunteered for babysitting duty. She hadn't wanted to bring her son with her this time. Not even when she knew that Bashir might be grateful for it. Protecting AJ was her top priority. Though he was too young to comprehend what had changed, she wouldn't disrupt his life any more. And she wouldn't let anyone else do it either.

As she thought this, she glared at Bashir and raised her chin. A silent challenge for him to say what he'd come to say. She was a big girl. Capable of handling herself if he backtracked on his decision to marry her.

"Can we have the room?" Bashir spoke, his eyes on her, his command for the other occupants in the room. "If that's all right with you?" he addressed her.

Tight-lipped, she stiffly nodded at her lawyer, dismissing her counsel just as Bashir sent his entourage away as well. Now, with the spacious conference room all to themselves, she locked her hands atop the table and stared back at him. He had to have a reason to drive everyone away. She was intrigued to hear it.

But not patient enough to wait.

"Are you having second thoughts?" She'd rather know now and get it over with, avoid any gallant effort on his part to soften the blow of rejection. Not that she would be upset or devastated. They weren't close enough to incite those feelings. She *did* need to know what he planned to do next if he wasn't going forward with the marriage of convenience.

He leaned back in his chair, his legs crossed, one hand plucking at his thick beard hairs and the other drumming his fingers over the tabletop. Like an island, the dark rectangular solid wood sat between them. He was so near, but his expression and thoughts were entirely out of reach. Without them, she was groping sightless in the dark, unclear as to where this would lead.

"I just need to know," Yusra said.

And she only breathed easier when he replied, "Nothing's changed. I only felt what had to be said should stay between us. We are the ones getting married. Speaking of marriage, shall we discuss our terms and expectations now?"

"That would be a good idea." She hadn't planned to agree to this without guidelines and contingencies for their marriage. They were two strangers who knew nothing about each other, and most couples in love still put all cards on the table. That way no party was surprised or hoodwinked, and the decision was as consensual as possible.

"Do you want to start first?" He stopped tapping his fingers over the table and fanned his hand at her, inviting her to take the lead.

"I guess we should begin with finances." A leading cause of why relationships fell apart. It hadn't been entirely why she and her ex-husband had broken up, but money had been an issue. Particularly as he'd thought she was making too much and somehow destroying his masculinity because her paychecks had more zeroes in them. But she didn't want to think of that, not when she was in the middle of negotiating her way into another marriage.

Yet, informed by her previous disaster of a relationship, Yusra highlighted her thoughts, "I won't quit my job." She wouldn't make the mistake of pleasing anyone again. She liked her job and shouldn't have to leave it even if her life would be changed by Bashir and his billions.

"I'm fine with you working."

"You live aboard your yacht, don't you?" She hedged, wondering if he understood what she was saying.

He nodded. "I do own homes though, throughout the world."

Homes. As in plural. She shouldn't have anticipated anything less, considering his immense wealth.

"What I'm getting at is that my work is here, in Kampala." She wouldn't leave Uganda. It wouldn't be fair of her to overturn her life and her son's when everything else was changing. Perhaps with time she'd reconsider, but right then she couldn't be convinced otherwise.

One big life decision at a time.

"I'm all right with that too," Bashir said. "Though that does bring us to our living arrangement. Where will we reside together?"

A little answering shiver zipped down her back like a bolt of lightning as she recalled her dreams of him. Vividly intimate dreams that seemed to feel more real every time she slept. No thanks to those dreams, she'd been fretting over having this conversation. Blushingly, Yusra accepted her attraction to Bashir, but she barred it from scrambling her good judgement. She just wanted to have both AJ and Zaire in her life; Bashir desired the same thing. That was it.

Channeling a calm she wasn't fully feeling, she said, "I was thinking we could swap homes. Spend the weekdays in Kampala, and the weekends on your ship."

"All of us?" Bashir's frown unnerved her. She wouldn't compromise about living on his ship full-time, but in fairness she was willing to work out the scheduling with him.

"I'd be willing to do Fridays on your yacht as well." And if work arose, she could take her laptop along and complete what she could from his vast floating home.

Still, even with this suggestion, his frown remained unchanged.

"Will that be a problem?" she ventured softly.

His scowling features grew fiercer. "Actually, yes. Zaire hasn't lived anywhere else."

In disbelief, Yusra exclaimed, "*What?* Why?"

Bashir had hoped to evade this question. He hadn't been bothered by his choice of lifestyle before. Soon after Zaire had come into his world, he'd purchased the megayacht and incurred the annoyingly costly maintenance of it for his peace of mind. His reasons for his unconventional lifestyle were simple: He had more control of his environment. Isolation meant less of a chance at risking accidents and the disquieting emotions that usually followed. For nearly three years he'd succeeded in protecting Zaire.

And protecting myself from losing him.

Bashir clenched his teeth at the mere thought of harm coming to his son. Keeping Zaire safe was all he'd wanted. And he had believed in his method.

Until now.

Until he sat opposite Yusra and watched inquisitiveness overtake her expression. She hadn't even heard his explanation and already she was beginning to look at him differently. Or that was what it felt like to him. Bashir supposed he also could just be overly sensitive. Seeing what wasn't there because that was what he expected. Her confusion. Her judgment.

Her objection.

Whatever the reason, it made it harder to discuss.

"I own homes and hotels the world over for when I have to travel for work. However, when Zaire was born, I quickly realized it wouldn't be fair of me to uproot his life every time my work called for it. It took some adjusting, but I work from and live on the yacht, and that arrangement allows me to be close at hand in case my son needs me."

"So, Zaire has lived all his life on the ship?"

Bashir's jaws ached from the pressure he applied. He relaxed his muscles enough to grit between his teeth, "Yes."

"You know that's going to have to change. It'll be a tough adjustment, but one that has to happen if we're going to make this *marriage* work."

Nothing in her tone suggested she pitied him or even held a shred of judgment against his parenting style. She was simply stating a fact. Both of their lives would have to change to accommodate their marriage and their family.

"Weekends on the yacht are fine then." Bashir didn't know what else to say. He was relieved that she hadn't judged him. He didn't know what to make of that. What to think *of her.* Most of all, Bashir didn't know whether to relish his good luck that of all people he had to be caught up in a baby swap with, that it was Yusra, or if he should worry that she would demolish his iron-clad defenses with her get-along-to-go-along personality.

Even now, when she smiled at him, he felt an inexplicable warmth all over. A heat that nestled most beneath his breastbone and around a certain vital organ.

Her smile only faltered when she spoke again. "My apartment's small though. It won't fit all of us."

"We'll look into a bigger apartment," he said breezily. Money wasn't an issue. He'd gotten over one of his biggest obstacles, telling her about his and Zaire's way of life, and trusting that she wouldn't scorn him. The rest was a cakewalk.

Or not.

Yusra's brows drew together in frustration. "Okay, but I'll help pay the bills. You're already providing AJ with a trust fund. I don't expect more money from you."

Ah. That was what this was about. Her financial independence.

To ease her mind, he said, "Zaire has a trust fund too. I don't want one of them to have what the other doesn't. And when both boys turn twenty, they'll have access to their money. It'll give them a safety net as they navigate new adulthood." And since they were on the topic… "What are your thoughts on a prenuptial?"

"Wouldn't that be a bad omen to the marriage?"

"A prenup would give you more power and choice ultimately. Although the other option is a postnuptial later on." He was fine with either alternative.

"Then let's wait. I don't want to doom this before it starts."

His heart pattered faster at that. She cared about this marriage, even though it was a means to an end for them both. And though it was important for him to solve their baby swap as bloodlessly as possible, it wasn't like him to open himself to possible legal problems. His lawyers wouldn't like him holding off on a premarital agreement. They would ask him to reconsider, and he'd remember this moment with Yusra and hesitate. Did he trust her enough to do what she asked and pause on the prenup?

Yes.

Decided on that, he moved past it before he questioned where his sudden strong trust in her had sprung from.

"There was something else I wanted to ask. Does AJ have a father figure in his life?" Bashir needed to know that he wouldn't be treading on another man's toes. Though he knew she'd been married before, he hadn't asked the private investigator to dig into Yusra's ex-husband who was also Zaire's biological father. It felt too personal.

Yusra shook her head. "He never met AJ, and he wanted it that way. He probably wouldn't even want Zaire."

"He's a fool."

Yusra smiled, but the ice in her gaze for the man who'd abandoned her and her son didn't immediately thaw. "What about you?" she asked. "Who do I have to thank for AJ?"

Bashir had known this time would come. He had asked her a personal question; now it was her turn to grill him. He'd just avoid mentioning his late cousin. "I didn't know AJ's biological mother well. She passed away shortly after giving birth to him."

That was all he'd give her for now. If he thought too hard of Imran he'd buckle under the pressure and tell her about his cousin. And he wasn't prepared for that. Not yet.

First, they had this marriage to commit to. And he had the perfect way to start their journey.

Bashir palmed his trouser pocket and the square-shaped object nestled inside for safe-keeping. Discreetly he pulled the item from his pocket and fisted its velvety-soft exterior. He didn't know if there was a better time to present it. They were alone. They were agreed on this marriage and they had gotten on the same page about most of the values that mattered.

Closing his fist around the small but significant box, he said, "That takes care of your job, living situation, finances. Anything else?"

...living situation, ...tell him nothing else.

So when she lowered her head in an act of unmistakable shyness, he couldn't quell his intrigue.

"There is one more thing," she said softly.

Bashir lifted his eyebrows, curiosity thickening. "Yes?" he prompted. What had they forgotten to discuss?

"It's about our living situation," she said, studiously avoiding his eyes. It took some serious dedication since he was sitting across from her and there wasn't anything of consequence in the room her lawyer had arranged their meeting in. Anything that could grip her attention more than he could.

"Yusra."

He hadn't meant to speak her name firmly and impatiently, but it had the intended result. She slowly met his eyes. Excruciatingly slow. Time could have stopped for centuries and he wouldn't have been able to tell when she enthralled him in her gaze.

"Intimacy," she squeaked.

"Intimacy," he growled.

"Are you expecting us to…um…*sleep together*?" She meant sex.

He'd thought of it too. But physical intimacy was too chancy. Too much of an uncertain variable he couldn't risk taking. Nere was an attracted he was to Yusra, and there was an attraction there—how could there not be? She was beautiful. And she would be his wife soon. Those two reasons alone were temptation enough.

"Would you like us to be physically intimate?"

"*No!*" she sputtered, right before she softened the blow to his ego with, "It would be too soon. Right? We're strangers."

"Agreed. Our marriage will be unique. I wouldn't expect for it to conform to the norm."

"But what if you change your mind? What if I do?" Her brows crumpled. "Unless there's an end date to this marriage."

"Not unless you'd like to end things. I don't intend to initiate a divorce."

"And you're perfectly fine with the possibility of no intimacy forever? Really?"

Bashir sobered and considered the gravity of what he was agreeing to do. A marriage—a tie that would bind him to her for the rest of his natural life unless she permitted otherwise—and with no promise of consummating the union. It would be a great sacrifice, knowing the pleasure sex could bring at the right time and with the right person. But he didn't know yet that this marriage would be right or that Yusra was that person for him.

But what if she is?

Bashir held back a groan as doubt assailed him. He couldn't do it. Couldn't close the door completely on their not being intimate ever.

"We can table it for discussion some other time," he said instead.

"All right," she relented quickly and with the barest hint of a warm smile. Almost as though she'd been thinking the same thing.

He hoped she had been because he'd feel less alone if she desired him too...

"Before we call the lawyers back in, there's something I have to show you." Loosening his nerveless fingers around the all-important box in his hand, he walked around to her side of the table and set the box down before her.

She goggled at it, giving a sharp intake of air when he snapped the lid open for her.

"A ring," she breathed.

Not just any ring. He'd had it customized in Greece by a reputable jeweler. A two-carat oval-cut central diamond encircled by smaller pavé diamonds and set on a white gold band. Cost hadn't been his problem. Rather he worried she might not like it and comforted himself that they'd search for a ring together if that was the case.

But he wanted her to like it. Wanted to know that he hadn't messed this relationship up right from the start, as he had with his late cousin's family.

He'd lost them without realizing it. And then he had lost Imran. He wasn't raring to make the same mistake a third time.

This marriage had to work. It had to last. He couldn't lose AJ, and to have AJ, he had to have Yusra.

So it wasn't a good sign that she hesitated to accept his ring.

"If it's not to your specifications, I'll book an appointment with the jeweler for you. You can take my jet—"

"Your jet?" she asked, her face awash with surprise.

"The jeweler's located in Greece."

"Bashir, I'm not going to Greece. Not for a ring." She looked down at the ring again, the brilliance of the gemstone gleaming in her eyes. "It is beautiful though, and it must have cost a fortune."

"Is that what's bothering you?"

She snorted indelicately. "You make that sound like it's not normal to worry about money. But no, it's not about the price."

"You don't like it," he said, trying not to take it personally.

"It's not that either."

"But there *is* a problem."

"There is, but I can guarantee it's not what you're thinking."

Bashir wouldn't know what to fix unless she told him. He studied her, searching for some hint as to how to repair the situation, but instead he was distracted by her loveliness. Again. Her hijab was a silky black that shimmered with her every movement. Her blouse and loose-fitted trousers simple and airy, sensible for the curtain of dry heat cloaking the city outside.

Engrossed by her, he nearly forgot he'd been waiting on an answer.

She gave him one finally. "The ring is beautiful, maybe too much so. That and, truthfully, all of this is just happening so fast—I know it has to, and I *want* to do this, but it doesn't make it easier."

"It's a big decision and a big change," he concurred.

Yusra smiled shakily, but still a smile was an improvement to her pleated brows and disheartened frown. She then flicked her glance from him to the sparkling diamond ring. Snagging her bottom lip with her teeth, she gave it a nibble, drawing this out, teasing him without intending to, before giving him what he desired.

"All right." Her smile more carefree, faint laugh

lines emerging around the corners of her entranc-ing eyes. "How do we do this?"

Galvanized into action, he pulled the ring from its temporary resting place and tucked the empty box away. Taking her hand gently, Bashir showed her exactly how. The ring slid down with ease, coming to a rest on her finger perfectly, as if it knew that it had found its forever home.

Looking away from the shiny new addition on her left hand and up to her face, he thought of telling her that the ring was most exquisite when she wore it. But that confession would be too much to say to her right then when they were still getting to know each other.

So he said the simplest and truest thing. "You're right. The ring is beautiful, Yusra, but perfectly so."

CHAPTER SIX

ALL YUSRA COULD think on the day of her wedding was whether she'd been this queasy and light-headed before her first marriage. Had it been like this with her ex?

She angled her handheld fan over her face and closed her eyes with a sigh. The air-conditioning in the building couldn't cool her stress sweat, and she wouldn't allow her full face of makeup to go runny before the day had truly begun. Although the wedding wasn't for another hour, she'd woken up early to go through the motions and prepare for the big moment when she and Bashir faced the imam in the traditional Islamic ceremony of nikah.

We're really getting married.

Her stomach clenched and her heart rate picked up as reality set in.

Rather than fall prey to her anxiety though, she redirected her thinking to her mental checklist. She'd gotten through makeup, her dress was waiting in the wings and she looked down at the henna on her hands, admiring both the ornate body art and the new manicure and pedicure she'd treated herself to at the last minute. That was all. She didn't have to worry about catering, guest service or anything else. Bashir promised her it would all be handled by his people. Even Zaire and AJ were in his care. The two toddlers had tuxedo sets for the special occasion. Yusra had seen them in their adorable outfits, and she was anticipating reuniting with them soon. The wedding itself was comprised of the religious ceremony followed by a party with a small and *exclusive*, as Bashir phrased it, guest list.

All she knew was her parents and siblings would be attending virtually on a large projector screen. She didn't want to do this without her family by her side, and Bashir had recognized that and made it possible for them to be with her. Yusra could feel herself smiling at his thoughtfulness even now.

So far, it was going swimmingly with him. He hadn't given her any cause to distrust him or her decision to agree to marry him. True, they had a long way to go to familiarizing with each other, but Yusra was optimistic that they would eventually settle into their relationship comfortably and companionably.

"Are you ready for the dress?" The makeup and dress personnel that Bashir had booked on Yusra's behalf had returned from their short break to finish what they had started early this morning.

Yusra nodded bashfully at the two women.

She was as ready as she could ever be. Ready to be a mother to AJ and Zaire.

And ready to be Bashir's wife.

Bashir stole glances at her from the side, not having gotten his fill of Yusra since she'd joined him in the small but tastefully decorated reception hall. At first it was to prove to himself that she was there, and she hadn't run off as he'd imagined she might. And then once he was certain that she was committed to seeing this through, he looked astonished at his wife-to-be's transformation.

She had been dressing modestly this whole time, and even though he had his suspicions that she'd glow up well, Bashir hadn't been sufficiently prepared to see her like this.

Yusra wore a *dirac*, a traditional ankle-length Somali dress. The outfit and its matching shawl were of a sparkling green-and-gold chiffon-and-satin silk. Her makeup was more noticeable, too, but only that her lashes were longer and darker, her cheeks rosier and her lips more tempting in that shade of rich cocoa brown. And her perfume—he inhaled as furtively as possible, drowning his lungs in the enrichingly sweet and peppery scent of her oud before stoppering it so that he could possess it. She smelled heavenly, and it was distracting him because the imam bored his eyes into him, clearly waiting for a reply to a question Bashir had missed.

"Could you repeat the question?" he grumbled with the annoyance that he'd been caught daydreaming.

The imam gave him an indulgent smile as if he knew why Bashir had been ensnared by his thoughts before asking him again to confirm the mahr or dowry.

If only he knew that this marriage was borne out of a selfish desire for him and Yusra to keep their children in their lives. And what he hadn't told her yet was that he also had the added pressure of bringing his nonprofit project to life without the media causing a field day with a scandalous baby swap. The only thing those vultures would love more would be discovering that his and Yusra's marriage was purely business. But nobody knew of this, not even Yusra's family.

From Yusra he knew that her neighbor and her lawyer were both aware of their circumstances, but he trusted her when she said that her neighbor wouldn't tell a soul, and her lawyer had an obligation to her client not to reveal sensitive information.

Like a marriage of convenience.

On his side, there were two other people who were aware of the true nature of his relationship with Yusra. Zaire's nanny Alcina, and his reliable aide Nadim. And he respected them enough not to insult their intelligence with lies. He hadn't ever brought a woman aboard his yacht before, and even when Zaire hadn't been in his life, he'd had very few romantic entanglements. None of those had become serious enough to warrant more than a paragraph or a hastily captured photo in a gossip rag. He had always believed he'd die a bachelor. His career kept him satisfied professionally, and the care he had for Zaire—and now AJ—was enough. He hadn't been interested in exploring romance or chancing love.

And he didn't have to do either with Yusra as she didn't want either herself. On paper and in person they were a perfect match.

Bashir held that closely in mind when he signed the marriage certificate after Yusra.

Then as witnessed by her family virtually, who Bashir had the briefest chance to speak to right before the ceremony began, and their other wedding guests, he and Yusra were officially declared wedded.

She's my wife.

He'd expected that outcome. What he hadn't

been ready for was the confusing delight that came with that realization.

After the *nikah* ceremony, the *walima*, or wedding banquet, moved over to an adjoining conference hall. The room was simply decorated with a backdrop of champagne-pink drapes, white-and-blush-pink roses and sprawling green ivy. Gleaming gold candelabra, charger plates and vases were their table decor. Bashir guided Yusra up the white floor runner to the head table. She had her hand secured from under his elbow with her fingers lightly gripping his forearm. If he weren't wearing a couple layers, she'd have felt him tense briefly at that first touch before relaxing into her, familiarizing himself with what this would be like from here on out.

We're actually married.

He didn't feel too different.

Except now he had more responsibility hanging over him. Because he wasn't caring for Zaire only, but for Yusra and AJ now as well. He had a whole family relying on him. As worrying as that was, Bashir took one look at his new wife's beaming expression and tabled the threat of panic lathering up in him. Once they were done celebrating with those who had come to witness their wedding, Bashir would have all the time to concern himself with how he'd have to conduct himself from that point onward.

Until death do us part.

They hadn't spoken those explicit vows, but they might as well have, as he'd already told her that he had no intention of divorcing her. Unless she asked him for it. But he wouldn't instigate it, no matter how bad it got. He hadn't arrived at this point in his life by making careless choices.

Marrying Yusra had been more than ideal.

Not that he needed a reminder, but if he did, all he had to do was peel his eyes off her beauty for a moment and look ahead of them at the head table. Waiting for them there were their sons. Alcina had managed to get the two hyperactive toddlers seated before congratulating the couple and leaving to snag her seat at the only other table set for their small wedding brunch.

Yusra fixed her smile on the children, her attention and love equally divided as they neared and the boys clamored to greet them. Bashir guided her around to her seat, pulling out her chair before grabbing the one beside her. AJ sat on her side, while Zaire sat on his. But that arrangement didn't last because his son kept looking around him, his eyes rounding with curiosity at Yusra. Without asking, Bashir hoisted Zaire onto his lap, and shifted so that Yusra could beam that sunshine-personified smile down onto her new stepson.

Zaire shyly interacted with her, his tiny hand reaching out to stroke his fingers over her cultural Somali dress. He did the same to her chandelier diamond-and-emerald earrings when she lowered her head closer to his level and he tapped at the dazzling jewelry. Her gold bangles were next, then he grew preoccupied with the red henna wreathing her hands. Finally, Zaire brushed a curious fingertip over her engagement and wedding bands.

Bashir's heart thudded faster. Not for the first—or he suspected last—time, he gazed at the rings in wonder too.

Three years ago, if asked whether he imagined himself ever marrying and having a family, he'd have guffawed with laughter. And why not? He had worked so hard to distance himself from any and all forms of love. Losing his family, and then the constant needling fear of losing the new family he'd discovered with Imran's parents and siblings and Imran himself, had left him scarred and irreversibly convinced that loving wholly and giving yourself to another would undeniably end in grief and heartache.

Some might call him lonely. Pathetic even. But at least his money was more of a likely constant. More so because he had been smart with investments, guaranteeing that he didn't put his eggs into one basket whenever he did make bold financial moves. And being in the hotel industry had assurances of its own. People always traveled and required accommodation. He had no worry about losing business.

Bashir had been happy being on his lonesome. Now he could only hope he'd be satisfied with this marriage.

"Are you happy?" he asked Yusra suddenly.

The press of her stare was heavy, contemplative. Then she blinked and her smile was as bright and warm as it had been for their children. "Yes." She looked down at the two small faces gazing up at her adoringly, totally smitten with her, and repeated, "Yes, I'm happy, Bashir."

He knew her contentment was due to the boys rather than because of him. But he didn't think an answer could be so perfect. It reinforced his belief their union could last if they avoided overwrought emotions that could only lead to anguish and heartbreak.

Yes, it's possible, Bashir thought confidently, while watching the family that was now his.

Zaire had climbed onto Yusra's lap, and AJ curled into her side and snuggled his head against her breast. She didn't fuss that they could be messing up her beautiful clothing or complain that their added body heat chanced melting her lovely makeup. Unfazed by their crowding, she gazed down at her sons with pure love in her smiling eyes.

Satisfied once more that he'd made the right choice with this marriage, Bashir stood and graciously addressed their small group of guests. They had this one last step before he and Yusra and their two sons started their new lives together.

"Do you want me to take them off your hands?" Bashir's pleasantly resonant voice sounded from beside her.

Yusra hadn't forgotten he shared the town car with her. Lifting her head from watching over the slumbering boys cuddled on both sides of her, she regarded him, understanding that this was her new life. This man, now her husband.

He had divested himself of his black silk bow tie, the first two buttons of his pleated-front dress shirt opened, and the collar parted so that her eyes couldn't miss the darkly brown swath of skin with its teasing hint of curling chest hair. Unbidden, her fingers tingled with the instinctual ache to stretch out and test if those hairs were coarse or soft to the touch.

Two hours into this marriage and I'm already messing up.

She chided herself, but even as she resisted her attraction to him, desire pulsed through her like a second, fluttery heartbeat. And it wasn't being helped by the narrowing intensity of his eyes on her. Could he read her mortifying thoughts about wanting to stroke his chest?

"They must be heavy," he observed in that even-tempered manner of his.

No, then. He hadn't clued in to her gutter mind.

"Your arms have to be hurting by now," he said.

He was correct. She barely had feeling left in them. They still had another ten minutes or so before they reached their hotel, so she wasn't too confident she could hold on to their sons comfortably until then.

Quietly, Bashir leaned in to help displace the weight of AJ and Zaire. He didn't have to stretch far to reach her. His firmly muscled thigh was already pressed to her leg, and she couldn't avoid the rest of him entirely. Bashir wasn't a small man. And she sensed that he knew that and was even pained by the fact that the world hadn't considered a person of his build and stature. But his tall height and muscular build weren't points against him. If they were, she wouldn't be so receptive to him every time he came near her, forget the few times they'd come into direct contact. Even her dreams were hopelessly affected by him. She'd been confident that her attraction to him wouldn't be a problem in this relationship.

She wasn't so certain of that anymore.

"There. Better?" Bashir asked after he settled AJ against him and helped her rest Zaire's head onto her lap instead.

"Much better," she said gratefully and with soft laughter. "Though I should get used to this. Raising one toddler's a handful—I'm guessing raising two will be a learning curve."

"You're not alone there."

She gave him a knowing smile, her insides feverish again the longer he gazed at her. Afraid that she'd reveal her attraction to him, and only after they had embarked on this loveless and highly convenient marriage, Yusra sought a new topic of focus.

And she found one.

"Who was that man who hugged you as we were leaving?" Considering Bashir had shown nothing but emotional reservation in the short time she'd known him, it had been shocking to witness him being embraced by one of their wedding guests. A short, rotund older gentleman who had been dressed snappily in a three-piece silver suit had approached Bashir, kissed him twice on the cheeks and bear-hugged and clapped him on the back. It had made her see her new husband in a different light.

"Otis Alexiou Doukas."

"That's not what I meant," she said, stifling a sigh.

Bashir stared back at her. "I know." She thought he even smiled, but it was hard to tell when he looked out his car window. "He was my business mentor back when I didn't have a business of my own. Otis gave me my first job. He took me under his wing and taught me the ins and outs of hotel management. And before that, he rescued me from rotting in a Greek prison when I was caught pickpocketing. I was young, not entirely bright, and angry at the world like most teenagers seem to be, yet Otis still lifted me up. Everything I have today, I owe in large part to him."

"You're fond of him," she surmised.

"He's been a big help to me, that's all. I appreciate what he's done."

"So, in other words, what you're *saying* is that you're *fond of him*." Yusra bit her lip to stop the laughter tickling her throat. Bashir gave her a brooding look, and it wasn't helping her losing battle to keep from laughing in his face. He just looked so worked up and confused and it was so dorky and adorable.

With a soft grumble, he said, "He insisted on coming to the wedding once I emailed him."

"He wanted to support you, just like my family did for me."

Bashir grumbled again. "I warned him it would be a quick ceremony and banquet. Nothing to clear his work schedule for and drop everything, family life included, to fly out from Athens."

"Bashir, just be happy he came. Clearly Otis cares about you."

She heard him mutter unintelligibly, but she smiled around his mock protest. In spite of the way he was acting, it was obvious that it had mattered to him to have his business mentor and friend present at their wedding. It was better than no one showing up to support him. Yusra had been intrigued when no family of his had been added to the guest list. So, she had done a little digging online. It hadn't taken too many search engine results to learn that Bashir lost his family. The details weren't clear in the articles she'd skimmed, only that they'd died in Somalia, and that he'd immigrated as a young teen to Greece after their deaths.

Yusra had stopped reading after that, her heart torn. She wanted to sob on his behalf, just as much as she wished to confess about snooping on him. Especially since she had a secret she hadn't shared with him. She still hadn't told him about being married before. Hiding her divorce wasn't ever a plan. It just happened. In the midst of everything else, she'd lapsed in telling him and now she didn't know how to disclose the secret she was holding. Feeling guilty again, she grew silent and pondering.

"Reconsidering the marriage already?" Bashir touched his wedding band. An austere solid white steel. Simplistic in design, but obvious in its symbolism. He was taken. Spoken for. Off the market. Smiling a rare smile, he said, "I was kidding."

"I know," she whispered.

It took a few bracing breaths to explain herself. "There's something I should have said to you earlier. I…was married before."

Oddly, he looked more uncomfortable than she did all of a sudden.

"Actually, I was already aware of that information," he said, voice noticeably gruffer. Careful not to jostle AJ, he shifted in the hot seat, and his discomfort only became more pronounced. "I hired a private investigator to look into you when I learned about the baby swap and AJ."

"What?" she hissed. She wouldn't wake up the boys, not even when Bashir floored her with his news.

Looking away from her, out of embarrassment or fear she didn't know, he divulged, "I had to know that AJ was being cared for properly."

"So you combed through my life? That's your excuse."

He grimaced and met her eyes. "I sincerely apologize. I know now it wasn't the most appropriate course of action, but it felt efficient to me at the time. And to be clear, I didn't look up your whole life. Just your finances, your business and your first marriage."

"So just most of it, great. I feel less violated. Thanks." After her sarcastic outburst, she stewed quietly to herself for a moment, and by the time she spoke again, she wasn't anywhere near as upset as she believed she'd be. And she knew why. "Since we're confessing, I looked you up too. I had to ensure you were a real billionaire."

He snorted.

Yusra grinned, but her good humor dampened when she remembered his family and his sad past. She chose not to mention his loss. She didn't think they were ready for that yet. Their relationship too new, their trust far too young.

"Guess that makes us even, but next time I think we should just ask and talk to each other whenever we want to know something," she advised with a sage nod.

"You mean like a married couple." Another precious smile from him.

Yusra rolled her eyes even as she laughed at his joke.

She didn't know what their future held precisely, but if they had more moments like this, they wouldn't do too badly.

We might even be happy together.

CHAPTER SEVEN

Yusra held on to her optimistic outlook as long as she could, but on the third morning of her marriage to Bashir, she accepted that something had to change or they'd be staring down the start of a long, depressive life together.

She would've spoken up to her new husband, but he was once again working the day away.

Which left her, AJ and Zaire stuck in their opulent suites at a well-known five-star luxury resort in Kampala. Not the worst place they could be trapped. Honestly, she wasn't even stuck in the hotel. Bashir hadn't locked her in their rooms or barred her from leaving. She could go visit her apartment. Go to work. Take the boys to enjoy some of the resort's amenities, like the pool or the butler service. Basically live life as normally as possible prior to their marriage. And she *wanted* to do all of that, but she couldn't help feeling as though Bashir hadn't yet embraced the significant change in his life.

We're married!

That had to have made him pause and think. Didn't he feel different? *She* felt changed. Since their nuptials, she'd woken up every day with a mixed bag of emotions. First the subtle realization whenever she felt the weight of her wedding rings on her finger, and then the quiet glow of satisfaction at having found a way to keep AJ and Zaire with her, which was closely trailed by the gnawing curiosity of what Bashir was up to *and* whether he was thinking of her in that moment too.

The curiosity always inspired distraction. And with distraction came frustration and the loss of concentration and patience for pretty much everything else in her life except for their sons.

"Good thing I'm on holiday from work then," she muttered to herself on that third, very early morning. While Zaire and AJ slept snugly and soundly, she'd risen for Fajr prayer, the earliest of Islamic prayers or salah. After praying, she started her day. There wasn't any point in returning to bed when she was fully awake and too alert for her own good. Even now, as she quietly padded from her bedroom to the living and kitchen areas of the hotel suite, Yusra's mind was stuck on Bashir.

So when she saw him, sitting in her usual chair at the long dining table, she did the only sensible thing. She froze every muscle. Blinked hard several times. And gawked at him openly until he noticed her.

"Good morning," he rumbled simply, his eyebrows lifting in question when she stood there unresponsive.

Had she summoned him with her thoughts?

She unrooted her feet, her fuzzy slippers silently carrying her over to him. For once he was forced to look up at her, though even then his imposing height nearly brought them to eye level. Yusra reached for him with a finger. She pushed that digit into the thick hardness of his shoulder. He didn't yield to her hard poke. When she jabbed at him again, he held aside the tablet he'd been poring over with one hand and trapped her wrist with his other big, warm hand.

"You're really here," she murmured.

He squeezed her arm, thumb flattening over the tender flesh of her inner wrist, against her jackhammering pulse.

"Where else would I be?"

"You're never here though," she retorted softly. "I've barely seen you since we arrived at the hotel."

At that accusation, Bashir released her. "It's been busier at work than usual. I hadn't anticipated it, otherwise I would have better accommodated for it prior to our marriage. But that's changed now. My schedule's clear for the next week." He stared at her for a clenching heartbeat, maybe more. She didn't know. Couldn't tell how long they gazed at each other in silence. Because though he wasn't touching her any longer, his eyes stroked over the whole of her as if he were, and wherever he looked, those parts of her body warmed. "You're not wearing your hijab."

She jerked her hand up to her head and, sure enough, no headscarf blocked her from running her hands over her veritable nest of 3C curls. Emphasis on the *nest*.

Oh, my God!

She backed away from him, flushed hot with embarrassment. Considering this was the first time he'd seen her hair, she must have made a disastrous impression.

Yusra cringed. Would it be too conspicuous of her to leave him and fix her hair?

"Your hair's shorter than I pictured," was all he said.

She touched her soft curls. "Is that bad?"

"No. It's cute."

Cute? She could live with cute. Before taking her seat and resisting the urgency to go fuss over her hair anyways, she made herself her typical breakfast. A bowl of maize porridge and two slices of toast. She noticed he'd helped himself to the coffee. But that was all.

There was a sumptuous breakfast spread of

Western and Ugandan dishes before him and his attention remained glued to his tablet.

Would he notice if I walked away?

She bet he wouldn't. It stung that he could be in the same room and still ignore her. If she'd known he'd be like this she would've asked him not to stay. And she certainly wouldn't have wanted him to spend time with her.

"Did I do something wrong?" Bashir's piercing gaze commanded her.

She swallowed, her throat giving a hard pull as tension trickled through her. "No... Why?"

"Unless I was mistaken, you were glowering at me."

"I was not!"

After a brief stare down, he resumed whatever he was doing on his tablet with absolutely no fight. Not even a whimper of protest. She wasn't worth any of that apparently.

"No, you're right. I lied. I was definitely glaring at you." She lowered her toast and brushed the crumbs from her hands once she had his focus again. "I did it because I'm annoyed. I've been cooped up in this beautiful hotel for days. And I know I'm not *actually* stuck here, but it feels like it when I sit around waiting for you to get back and, I don't know, talk to me. Maybe acknowledge that I'm here? I get that this isn't a normal marriage by any measure, but we're partners in a way. Right now, it feels like I'm doing this alone, and I don't like it. If I'd known it would be like this, I might not have agreed to it."

Bashir placed his tablet facedown. "I'm sorry."

"It's fine," she said, her cheeks the hottest part of her body right then. She blushed terribly. Her only saving grace being that he couldn't see the shift in mood in her. Without her annoyance, she only felt the mortification of having been so open and up-front with him.

But it's for the best.

She couldn't have bottled it a second longer if she had tried.

"No, it's not fine. I should have explained the demands of my work schedule. It won't happen again. Next time, I'll keep you updated."

She didn't know what else to say to that but, "Thanks."

Bashir settled his hand over the tablet. "May I show you something?" After she bobbed her head shyly, he got up and walked over to her and angled the screen so she could see whatever it was he wanted her to see.

"What am I looking at?" Yusra didn't recognize the thickly lush forest or the slender strip of river.

"Hopefully where we'll be for the remainder of the week. Assuming you're not too upset to spend a holiday with me."

Understanding clicked into place. "Was that what you were looking at this whole time?" Her humiliation skyrocketed when he nodded. Here she was believing the worst and going off on him when all he'd been doing was securing a vacation for them.

She groaned and covered her face. "I can't look at you."

Bashir's chuckle rained down over her. The throaty and sinfully sexy noise tickled her curiosity and she braved a peek up at him. Her breath snagging when she saw he was far closer than he had been a moment earlier. A strong sense of déjà vu slammed into her. They'd been in similar positions before, back when she had first met him in her office, and she'd gotten vertigo from her diabetes.

She felt dizzy now too. Only this time it had nothing to do with her blood sugar level.

Her skin felt hot and itchy and far too tight to contain her bones and sloshing blood. Her ears grew dull with the steady drumming beat of her heart. And her mouth had gone unreasonably dry on her. She licked her lips and breathed shakily when Bashir's stare dropped down to her mouth almost hungrily.

She swore desire roughened his voice as he asked, "Are we good on the holiday?"

"We're peachy," she chirped with the little air

she had left in her. She hadn't kissed or touched him, and it felt like she'd done both and more. It was a baffling reaction after harboring irritation for him.

Did she want him or want this marriage to work? Because instinct and her failed first marriage warned that she couldn't have both. The whole reason she believed her relationship with Bashir could survive was that they weren't in it for love. They were in this together for their sons, their family. So it was either she risked ruining it with her attraction to him, or she fought to make their marriage work for them.

She had an awful sinking sensation that only time would reveal what she would do.

Mosquito bites, a mild stomach bug and stepping into the steaming, fresh droppings of what could either have been a chimpanzee or a redtailed monkey, according to their tour guide, had been all the things that had happened to Bashir on four out of five days of their holiday.

What hadn't happened was another romantic moment between him and Yusra.

Which he should have been thrilled about. And he was, but it also didn't stop him from mulling over witnessing her desire for him. There had been no hiding it. She'd wanted him that day he'd told her about the holiday in their hotel suite. If he hadn't refocused the moment, she might have kissed him.

Or I could have kissed her.

Bashir hadn't been immune to her, just more concerned that if they were to stroll down that path, they'd have a hard time returning from it.

So avoiding any romance on this arguably romantic holiday had been his second objective.

His prime goal had been fulfilled: Yusra and their sons were enjoying themselves immensely.

And with one full day left before they journeyed from Jinja, Uganda back to Kampala, Bashir had a good feeling that his second goal was within reach as well. Especially for what they had planned for their final day.

White water rafting in the Nile didn't inspire the excitement of romance. No one proposed on dangerous rapids, Nile or no Nile. They would be moving too fast to risk kissing without chipping a tooth or two. And they'd be too busy holding the grab ropes and gripping onto their paddles for any chance at embracing. The only thing that would make it truly perfect in his eyes was if they weren't at the mercy of choppy waters.

"Are you ready?" Yusra gushed beside him, her face aglow with unbridled exhilaration.

She actually squealed when their instructor and guide hyped them up as they pulled away from the safety of the shore.

Bashir groaned. What inner beast in her had he released? But he could do nothing but grin and bear it when she looked damn adorable wrapped up in her bubble of oblivious enthusiasm. He was doing this so she had a happy experience. Why? He had asked himself that multiple times over since they'd begun their holiday. Finally, he understood there remained a part of him that worried Yusra would wake up one morning and decide this marriage wasn't good for her anymore. And then she'd take AJ with her, and he'd be back where he started, only this time with no other recourse if their convenient relationship ended.

He wouldn't lose her. He'd worked too hard for too long and burdened himself with too many sacrifices to risk another loss in his life. Because it would be a loss in a way. And not being with her meant forfeiting AJ and that wasn't acceptable. He would even sign up for several more white water rafting excursions to avoid that displeasing possibility.

Of course Bashir wasn't racing to volunteer anytime soon.

As he'd expected, the journey down the volatile midgrade rapids was nauseating to say the least.

He hadn't held on to anything so tightly in his life, but the grab rope became more than a safety line, it grounded him as he tore through the most intense sections of the river. He paddled when the guide called for it, and he wedged his feet into the thwarts whenever their raft slammed into the tallest of the white waves or squeezed past gaps between hazardous rocks. It wasn't exactly a death trap, and yet he still envisioned scenarios where things could go wrong. They could tip over the raft and get trapped beneath it. Or slam hard into the rocks and injure themselves badly. And those were only some of the ways this could end on a horrible note.

Strangely, there were points where his tension ebbed and a surge of endorphins dulled the ache in his calves and arms from holding on to the raft's supports.

It happened first when Yusra called to him and pointed out a pair of white-breasted birds mid-flight. They flew past them ahead, giving him a hopeful sign that the endpoint wasn't too far off.

The second time he looked back at her, she wasn't paying him any attention. Her bottom lip was caught between her teeth and she was struggling to help steer them away from a tricky rock that even the guide had missed. She pushed hard, but it wasn't enough, and her side of the raft tipped up as it climbed the rock.

The other six guests in the raft and the guide all noticed.

Everyone scrambled to right them.

All except Bashir.

He watched Yusra's water shoes slide out of the raft's foot cups and her hands tighten on her paddle to no avail. Her body jerked in the opposite direction of where the raft had climbed on the rocks, and she flailed an arm to right her balance.

Bashir sprang into action. He seized her arm and yanked her toward him, hard. She slammed into his chest, her forehead bumping his chin and his beard softening the impact of that blow. But she was safe. Jolted and possibly bruised, but no victim to the thrashing waters ferrying their raft farther downriver. The frenzy of the moment itself was packed into a handful of seconds, though it might as well have been hours for the burn consuming his lungs and the prickling fire scorching his muscles.

Bashir drew her onto his lap more, sitting back as comfortably as they could as the raft jostled free of the rock it had climbed and they crashed back into the river safely. And once again, they were moving along, the guests cheering around them for having overcome that challenge together. It didn't matter to him that he hadn't been of any help to them. Yusra had needed someone. And he'd been there for her. Prevented her from getting hurt…and him from having to deal with her injury or loss.

The thought of her in pain wrenched his heart.

Bashir clutched her closer since he couldn't palm his chest and ease the ache any other way.

He peeled her back from him once his heart rate steadied and she wasn't trembling. Wide eyes beheld him, her mouth parted slightly, and her chest rising and falling with her quickened breaths. He bet she had questions. And since he didn't have answers, at least any answers he felt comfortable sharing right then, Bashir welcomed any distractions.

"Is everyone all right?" The guide called, seeming to notice they weren't manning their areas of the raft.

Perfect, he thought.

Grasping their cue, Bashir released his gentle hold on her arms.

But it was Yusra who moved away first, her hands back on her paddle, and her eyes still searching his face, seeking an explanation he couldn't give her that moment.

And that he didn't know if he'd ever be able to give her.

As a reward for completing their white water rafting experience, their guide urged them to take an hour to relax in the shallower pools where they ended their expedition of the famed Nile.

Bashir was just glad it was over. He'd have remained on the shore and observed everyone else happily, but Yusra walked up the rocky riverbed and onto the sticky shoreside with an outstretched hand for him. Like the other travelers with them, she'd been swimming in the river, calling out to him to join her. She finally tired of waiting and came to fetch him.

"Come on. You can't stand there and watch the whole time."

He could, but he didn't say that to her. It wouldn't do him any good. Bashir might not have known her long, but he was quickly learning to accept her tenacity.

Compelled by the eager glint in her eyes as well, he took her smaller hand in his and marveled at the strength with which she pulled him along. Almost as if she was afraid he'd change his mind on her at the last moment and not wanting to take that chance she was instead risking ripping his arm out of its socket. She stopped tugging him along when the river waters hit her waist.

Waist-deep for her wasn't the same for him. He had more than a foot on her, so he was spared the difficulty of a wade. The warm water pooled around his upper thighs, his board shorts and black leggings soaked along with his rash vest, but that had happened long before they'd stopped as a group to soak in the calm parts of the Nile.

Like he had, Yusra had come prepared in bathing attire. She had on a long-sleeved swim top over a bodysuit and ankle-length swim leggings. Her pullover hijab had been a good choice, never having slipped off during their rocky ride downriver. And when it was all put together, she looked good.

Maybe a bit too good, he thought with a quickly drying mouth.

The modesty of her waterproof wear still conspired to undo him whenever his prying eyes tracked over her shapely curves and the generous swells of her breasts. He'd felt all of her when she had been pressed into him, shielded from the angry rapids of the river, but not protected from him. His hands flexed involuntarily at the memory of holding her enticingly soft warmth. If they'd been alone on the raft, things might have turned out differently. He could see himself crumbling to the temptation his wife embodied and stealing a kiss.

They'd been married for over a week, and they hadn't even kissed yet.

If they'd been a normal loved-up couple, he'd be worried. But his concern was unfounded. They hadn't married for love, or for kisses or any kind of intimacy for that matter. So he shouldn't be keeping score of how long he'd gone without testing his theory that her mouth was as soft and sweet as it appeared.

"I forget how tall you are sometimes," she said and, taking his wrist, pulled him along farther into the still river waters. "There. Much better." She beamed up at him once he was submerged at the waist, and with the water up to her chest now. "Let's swim together. You know how to swim, right? I can teach you. When I lived in Somalia, my home was next to Liido Beach. I used to swim there with my brothers and sister all the time."

"That's not it. I know how to swim." He stroked his beard and shifted his weight from foot to foot, the soles of his water shoes keeping him upright. "I'm not fond of water." Again, a flurry of questions brightened the dark, mesmerizing pools of her eyes. This time he had to give her something. When he'd held her on the raft and hesitated to let her go, he didn't know how to explain his actions. But this, *this* he could. It wouldn't be easy though, and it'd require trust in her. Trust not to belittle his feelings primarily.

Clearing his throat, he said, "When I immigrated to Greece, I journeyed over land…and by sea."

"You did *tahriib*." The word was spoken quietly, her tone tortured...for him?

Tahriib was the practice of bribed smugglers persuading unknowing migrants on a dangerous journey to Europe. For some, it delivered the intended result of reaching a promised land where opportunities for jobs and good money abounded, but for others, it ended in injury and at its worst even death.

He had been luckier than those who had lost their lives or found nothing but more pain in a new and strange land.

But if he stopped to think of them, he'd never get this story out fully. "During the journey itself, we stopped several times. The last leg was a long trip over the Aegean Sea from a coastal city in Turkey. It had been dark and stormy. We couldn't see anything as we were buffeted by high winds and tall waves." Bashir swallowed down the bile that rose with the memories. "Our raft's engine was torn off by the winds or waters—we didn't know, but we lost it, and we were left floating, helpless. Then the boat capsized."

Drowning had become no longer a terrifying possibility, but a reality.

"At that point in life, I couldn't swim. I'd never learned how to, and never imagined I'd require it. But once I fell in the sea, I lost consciousness quickly and blessedly. I wouldn't have wanted to remember the harrowing journey my body made from sea to land." Later, he'd been informed by a coast guard who had been on the rescue that there had been a dozen drowned souls scattered on the shore beside Bashir. He shuddered even now at the thought of being surrounded by death. Just like he'd been with his family. But he wasn't finished telling Yusra all of it. "Those of us who survived were cared for and then sent to await our fates in a refugee camp."

After that, he'd taught himself to swim the first chance he got.

"Learning to swim kept me occupied that first summer in the camp," he explained.

"Bashir, that's awful." She slid her hand in his, small, soft fingers squeezing support into him. "We don't have to swim. Let's skip rocks on the river's surface instead. Or we could take pictures of the birds if the rocks aren't a good idea." She pointed to the white-breasted birds that they'd seen earlier. The ones who'd outraced them to this tranquil location. A flock of them herded on the opposite shore. Against the backdrop of the dark green forest, the birds were like flecks of white flicked onto an opaque canvas.

Rocks. Birds. It was all the same to him though. An excuse to avoid a thing he didn't like—a thing he even feared, rightfully so. But he'd been scared to tell her what had been on his mind, and his trust in her hadn't steered him badly. Now his intuition promised that he wouldn't be wrong to trust her with this too.

"No, let's swim," Bashir said.

Her radiant smile was certainly worth braving a dip in the river.

"Were you waiting long?"

Yusra startled at the sound of Bashir's voice in the enclosed space.

She looked over her shoulder at the opening to the pop-up bubble tent. Golden fairy lights lined the tent's sturdy fiberglass frame and the transparent fabric shielding them from mosquitoes. He sealed the tent closed after him before one of the little bloodthirsty bugs snuck inside, but not before she felt the balmy kiss of summer's night air on her face and the soles of her bare feet. Having arrived earlier than he had with their sons, she'd kicked off her shoes, the floor of the tent covered by a handwoven, vividly dyed and patterned Persian rug. Before her was a low wooden table adorned with a colorful hand-sewn runner, although they could hardly see it under the crush of dinner plates. Two divans draped in the same decorative and delicate handmade tapestry as the table runner faced each other and provided more than enough room for their family of four.

She shared one of those floor sofas with AJ and Zaire. Bashir grabbed the sofa opposite them.

"Sorry I'm late. I hadn't expected to be tied up for as long as I was, but construction is in progress, so I'm on alert more than I'd usually be." He had been right behind her on their way to dinner in this cozy, well-lit tent when his phone had rung and he'd taken a call from his aide Nadim. He'd sent her along with the boys with a promise to catch up. But it had been a while since then, and she hadn't wanted to eat without him, so she had asked the resort's staff to bring plate warmers for everything.

As they uncovered the plates now, and began to eat, Yusra ventured, "A new hotel?"

"No, a nonprofit organization for migrants and refugees. It's called Project Halcyone."

That warranted her washing down the tenderized and well-seasoned chicken in her luwombo dish with freshly made passion fruit juice to clear her mouth and congratulate him. Though she was confused. This was the first she was hearing about his altruistic project.

Reading her thoughts, he said, "I didn't tell you because construction started three weeks ago, and I'm still waiting for it to feel real. I've been envisioning this project for some time now. I can only hope it will help as many people who need its services as possible once it's up and running." His stare grew hard and distant, and she recognized it from earlier. When they'd been in the river and he had told her about his perilous *tahriib* and the deadly consequences for some of his other travel companions.

She hugged their sons, their warm, small bodies staving off the chill brought on by her darkening thoughts. Holding them always did the trick in righting her mood. And she'd missed them for much of the day. AJ and Zaire had spent the time apart from her and Bashir with nanny Alcina. They'd been too young to go white water rafting with them, and given how the day had gone, Yusra was relieved for their absence. By the end of it, Bashir had gotten real with her. And some of that realness had taken them to a darker, grittier point of his past.

"It seems ambitious, but it always helps if your heart is in the right place. And yours is." She sensed Bashir needed this almost as much as the people he would be helping with his generosity. Still, it didn't take the sting of surprise away at discovering he was undertaking such important work. And she wondered whether *this* was the real reason why he'd proposed marriage to her. It wouldn't be the first time she had married a man who hadn't been completely forthcoming with her. With her ex-husband, it had taken her years to discern his little barbed comments about her job and salary, her homemaking skills and even her modest outfits. Yusra hadn't been enough for him in so many ways, and instead of telling her he was discontented with her and their marriage, he'd strung her along and wasted her hope, efforts and time on him. She'd tried to save their marriage by satisfying him, and only made herself unhappy along the way. She wouldn't do it all over again with Bashir.

She'd been about to resign herself to quietly worrying when Bashir shocked her again—this time with an apology.

"I should have told you earlier. Truthfully, I was concerned about the problem with the hospital." He looked from her to their oblivious sons. AJ and Zaire were busy playing with their food, their fists caked in deep-fried bread. Yusra had showed them how to eat the *mandazi*, but to no avail. Almost as much of the fluffy crumbs ended up on their faces as on their hands. Giving up, she allowed them to explore, barely flinching when their sticky hands pressed onto her belted maxi dress and shimmery abaya.

A testament to how focused she was on Bashir. She didn't want to miss what he had to say.

"I didn't know you, and therefore I wasn't sure what kind of person you'd be. I couldn't expose the nonprofit to any scandal."

"I can't fault you for that." She masked her

hurt behind a false serenity, censuring herself for being so weak. Everything he said made sense. If she, too, had a big project underway, she'd want to do anything to protect it. And to be fair, she hadn't trusted him all that much at first either.

I don't even have complete faith in him now.

She of all people understood trust was forged through incontestable actions, the louder the better. That was why she asked, "Do you view me as a threat now?"

Bashir rolled his shoulders, his large muscles flexing under his collared shirt and stylish seersucker blazer. The tension coming from him didn't inspire confidence that she'd like what was coming. "I'm not yet sure. For that I'd have to know you better. Before today, I didn't take you for the adventure-seeking type. White water rafting?" He shook his head with a pleasing tilt to those thickly rounded lips of his. "Should I be glad I didn't let you talk me into bungee jumping?"

She flung him a grin full of her relief and humor. "Then that's our problem. We still haven't gotten to know each other." And she knew one surefire way to remedy that. "When we head back to Kampala, we should go out, just the two of us."

"Are you suggesting we date?"

"No more than this holiday of ours can be construed as a honeymoon."

Bashir laughed briskly. "I can't argue with that logic."

Yusra's laughter came easily at that. This was a much better start to their marriage than those first few days she'd spent sequestered in their hotel suite, waiting, and wondering if marrying him had been an error of judgement on her part. It wouldn't have been her first mistake when it came to choosing a life partner. But now she felt less of that pressing concern for their still so new relationship. She told herself that it was for the good of Zaire and AJ for their parents to get along. This dating business was merely a sacrifice, one of countless she'd have made to safeguard their family. Meanwhile she pretended not to feel Bashir's smile and sparklingly dark eyes warming her from head to toe, and inside and out.

CHAPTER EIGHT

As FAR AS first dates went, this was the most unusual one Bashir had been on, and for more reasons than how he'd come to find himself on the back of a motorbike, clinging to Yusra while she navigated her city's traffic like a pro.

But he was also dating his wife.

Most of what they'd done so far had been out of order. Their family existed before their marriage, thanks to the baby swap ordeal. And they had barely known each other before agreeing to marry. Why did this have to be any different?

At least the honeymoon came after the marriage.

Honeymoon? When had he begun to see their holiday the way Yusra had, as a honeymoon rather than a simple vacation?

Bashir had obviously underestimated her influence on him. It likely wasn't any help that they'd spent the last week together in close quarters. Recognizing that she was sensitive to him working late away from her and their sons and wanting her to remain happy with her decision of marrying him, he had set up a second office from their hotel suite. In a short time, Yusra's satisfaction became as vital as Project Halcyone was to him. He told himself that he needed her cooperation for their convenient relationship, and though he knew that was partly true, it wasn't the whole truth. But he was resisting exploring what that meant. It'd be a danger to court any emotion around her. Affection for Yusra was a thing he couldn't risk. Because then he would grow to care for her, and *that* he wouldn't chance for the entire world.

Squeezing his arms around her a little more, he concentrated on the sights zipping past them. He'd seen parts of Kampala already. But not like this. Not at the total mercy of Yusra when he'd chosen to climb on the bike behind her. She was in control, keeping them upright and alive, and that was something new to him. Considering he'd spent most of his life caring for himself, and in so doing using his wealth to build the kind of life and world he wanted to live in, Bashir understood that this was more than a ride for him. He trusted her with his well-being. And that was significant for him. It would be important to her too if she knew what he was thinking, but that would require him telling her, and he wasn't inclined to do that. It would create a bond between them. The kind that wasn't easily broken or given up. The sort that would develop into deeper feelings and manifest even stronger ties to her.

Would that be such a bad thing?

With a frustrated grunt, Bashir narrowed his eyes at their surroundings, blurring past sometimes, and slowing down when confronted with bumper-to-bumper traffic.

"Is something wrong?" Yusra asked with a glance over her shoulder at him.

She'd heard him. Just how loud had he grunted?

"Fine." He gritted the word out as she gave a little wiggle of her rear. She was merely adjusting in her seat, but it dealt a catastrophic reaction in him. He felt himself go hard quickly, and with every little brush of her, she melted his control.

Focus on the date. On the views.

Yes, that was what he needed to do. Appreciate what he was experiencing. Starting with how he liked the city's liveliness.

More than the feeling of her in my arms?

No! He clenched his jaws fast and hard, biting back at that disruptive thought. But Allah help him, the fiendish vibrations of the bike were like oil deliberately poured over a fire and then onto him. Whenever he attempted to shuffle away from her, the bike engineered them back together. He couldn't escape the bike's teeth-chattering, full-body quake, just like he was forced to accept that he'd be pressed against Yusra until they stopped. He muffled his instinctive groan when she drove the bike a little faster and her softly rounded backside rubbed along his front. She molded there so damn perfectly that he questioned whether the universe was taunting him.

It's my fault!

Bashir had no one else to blame. He'd seen how small the motorbike was: that it would barely hold the both of them, with him taking up most of the space. He had warned her that it wouldn't be a comfortable ride, and that it might not be possible for them to do it together.

Yusra had dismissed his objection. "The bike can hold the two of us, and I'll even promise not to let you fall off," she'd said with a teasing wink. That had done it for him.

And now he was reaping the reward of his inability to see this far into the future.

That was how the remainder of his ride with her continued. With him striving to cut off all feeling to the lower half of his body, starving out his desire for her, and with her calling out different landmarks in that cheery voice of hers. There was the Uganda National Mosque, the largest masjid in not only Uganda but among those in East Africa. The palace of the Kabaka, a king, of the regal Baganda people of Uganda, along with the tombs of four previous kings in the Kasubi Royal Tombs.

She mentioned some other landmarks. None of which he remembered because he was preoccupied with slamming the brakes on his libido.

So when they finally came to a blessed stop, Bashir could have kissed the solid dry road beneath the soles of his shiny loafers.

He leaped off the bike as though the seat scalded him.

"Was that really your first time riding a *boda boda*?" Yusra unstrapped her helmet and hooked it over one of the bike's handlebars before straightening her two-piece hijab over her head.

"I avoid unnecessary danger." Where would Zaire be if Bashir were to have gotten into an accident on a motorbike? Even before his son had come into his life, he'd avoided thrill-seeking escapades, having had his fill of near-death experiences when he'd almost drowned at sea.

"Well, I just thought with you being a billionaire…"

"I'd be more reckless?"

She shrugged laughingly. "Is that terrible of me to think that way?"

"No, not terrible. More predictable than anything."

With another silvery laugh, she steered him away from the motorbike she'd rented for the day and toward the white stone building ahead of them. Its roof gleamed a deep-baked reddish brown in the afternoon sun; its expansive green grounds teemed with lounging people.

"My alma mater, Makerere University," Yusra told him when she noticed his focus shifted. "I studied arts here five years ago. Unless you know that already."

"Why would I know that?" He snapped his head down to her, puzzled before it dawned on him. "I didn't look into your educational background." It had only mattered to him that she could care for AJ, and he had felt guilty enough nosing into her life that he'd simply gleaned what he truly desired from the PI's report on her.

"Relax, I was just messing with you," she said with a smile.

He harrumphed, his face warmer all of a sudden and his chest tighter. Belatedly he understood he was blushing. Her harmless teasing had his mind reeling a bit more than it ought to have. Normally, people acted playful when they were comfortable with each other.

When they liked one another.

Did that mean she liked him?

And why did that insinuation perk up all his nerve endings?

Eager to redirect their conversation back to easier ground, he asked, "Why this school? Why

Uganda for that matter? I know Somalia has a few higher education institutes."

"During university, I did a school exchange for two semesters while studying fine arts in Somalia, and I got the chance to come to this city. I fell in love with it pretty quickly after that and never left. It helped that I qualified for a full-ride scholarship to Makerere to complete my studies." A sadness marred her beautiful features. "It was also around that same time I met my ex-husband."

Bashir's interest was piqued, and a sudden passion to know her more took hold of him. Even if that meant he had to sit through hearing about the man who'd left her and AJ to fend for themselves.

They walked along the length of the campus grounds, the chatter from the students milling on the green drifting over to, but not penetrating, their heart-to-heart.

"Guled was different back then. He was kind instead of cruel. After, the love he'd once shown me changed into contempt and resentment. By the end of our relationship, I didn't recognize him as the man I'd fallen in love with. We met here at the university. He used to work as an administrative aide at the student counseling office, and he had been assigned my case when I was in the process of transferring to study in Kampala."

"He's Somali too?" Bashir still found it odd

that of all the women who had to be tied to him through an accidental baby swap, that it was Yusra, and that she was Somali like him. And when she nodded, he murmured, "Small world." Because it really was a freakish case of fate.

"We clicked instantly, so when he asked to show me around the school and city, it was an easy choice. We dated for two years, and a month after I'd graduated, we got married and moved in together."

"So two loves kept you here. Your art, and him."

Yusra stopped him with a hand. "I'm not in love with him anymore, Bashir." Her fingers squeezed his arm lightly, impressing upon him that she had no lingering feelings for the man who'd come before him.

Deep down it shouldn't have made a difference to Bashir whether she still held a torch for her ex-husband or not. Because it wasn't like anything could happen between him and Yusra. They'd been open about that much. She wasn't seeking love from him, and he had thought that part was the sweetest end of their deal. He had enough on his plate. Zaire and AJ. His nonprofit. And how to live with a wife he shouldn't desire nor love.

That was plenty for him to handle without adding more.

And yet Bashir still gazed down at Yusra and, before her darkly long lashes, sunlit brown eyes and glossy lips bowled him over, said, "He really was a tremendous fool."

Though was he any less foolish for allowing his heart to thump faster when she beamed an approving smile up at him?

Showing Bashir her university should have been the highlight of the day. This place was where her life in Uganda had started, and in a way, it had brought her AJ. Well, Zaire technically, because that was who Guled and she had conceived. Though without Zaire, she wouldn't have been at the hospital giving birth to him, where AJ had been at the exact same time, and the baby swap wouldn't have eventually thrown her on a path to meeting the man who'd become her second husband.

But the truth was she had too many highlights from that day she planned to label as happy memories and squirrel away in her mind. From the ride through the city on a *boda boda*, to stalking her old campus grounds with him, and now strolling the city streets like a normal couple. They were even holding hands!

But that's only because it's crowded.

That was partly correct. She hadn't wanted to lose him. But just as strongly, she wanted to touch him again. And she hadn't been above using any excuse to do it.

Innocently unaware of her true motive, Bashir had accepted her hand and didn't speak up when she had interlocked their fingers, their palms connected, and she couldn't be happier in the moment. They were getting along. And he was being nice and thoughtful and everything she had once dreaded he wouldn't be. Sure, she hadn't felt as certain about them when he had been bounding off to work and ignoring her, but he'd changed since their holiday-cum-honeymoon. Relocating his office from his yacht to their hotel suite, carving out healthy time in his schedule to spend it with her and their sons.

They were two weeks into their marriage now and the forecast was looking rosier with each new day. Not that it made an impact on her decision to refrain from romanticizing their relationship. With her first marriage, she'd actually been in love, and it hadn't ended well for her. So taking that logic, this second marriage had more of a chance to succeed in the absence of love.

And maybe that was why it was working so well between them.

She knew he hadn't been interested in romance either. It should have been a solace to her to know she wouldn't be forced to be intimate with him. Bashir was perfect for her in that way.

So, why am I sad?

It didn't take her long to land on a plausible

theory. By choosing this marriage, she had given up on love, and that was why melancholy visited her suddenly. She was sad because she was shutting the door to ever falling in love again. Not just temporarily, but for forever.

And as long as she remained married to Bashir it would stay that way.

She didn't know what unsettled her more, that she had no hope of loving and being loved again, or that her gut twisted painfully in response to her picturing leaving Bashir. If it hurt her to think of that scenario, what did it mean?

Rescuing Yusra from spiraling deeper into her thoughts, Bashir gave her hand a squeeze and a tug before he pulled her to a gentle halt.

"Where's that?" He squinted at the distance, his lips pressing together firm and grave.

Yusra followed his line of sight to the Katanga slum. She must have grimaced loudly because he regarded her sharply.

It wasn't the first place she'd have shown him. Even for those who were braced for the poorest parts of the slum neighborhood, the poverty could be a hard experience to cope with. Even Bashir with his past as a refugee and the horrors of his *tahriib* might find it a difficult place to visit. And the last thing she wished to do was remind him of what he'd gone through.

Stretching for a mile, and bordered by the university and a sprawling hospital campus, the Katanga slum was a mixture of student hostels and impermanent mud-and-timber dwellings. A sea of rusted tin roofs covered narrow access roads and the poor drainage systems to those living in the area. There were already thousands of homes packed into the small parcel of land, and with many more people seeking shelter all the time, driven there by everything from poor choices in life to an inflated economy and unfeeling landowners and property developers.

"Katanga slum. It's a well-known settlement in the city."

"Is the government not doing anything to help them?"

"They try, but there are landowners involved. Figuring out who owns what part, and what they're owed is difficult to tell. At least that's what I understand." Yusra thought it so sad. She hadn't come from a rich background either, but she'd had what she had needed growing up. Even now, her parents and siblings tried to help in whatever way they could, with money, or small gifts. She could rely on them if she ever had the need to leave the home she'd built in Kampala, and she always remembered she was fortunate for that alone. Not everyone had someone in their corner.

Looking at Bashir, she recalled he'd lost his entire family.

She looked from him to the slum that she knew had to pain him to see. It wasn't what she wanted him to remember of this date, and not when everything had been going well.

"I thought we could visit the market next," she wheedled in the softest voice she could.

His hand tensed in hers. "It looks like the camp I lived in for four summers. Chaotic, crushed with people and tents and with no definitive lines as to what belonged to you. Stealing happened frequently. Food and drink and bedclothes were all fair game if you looked away and didn't protect what was yours. The security guarding the camp never did anything to help. And the weather? Unbearably scorching during the days. I can't tell you how many sunburns I'd accidentally peeled, tossing and turning in my sleep. The nights were the opposite. Cold even in the summer sometimes. Cold enough for my chattering teeth to keep me awake."

Yusra listened to it all, her stomach bunched in knots for him, a sickness swelling in her for what he'd gone through, and when he'd been so young. The article she had read claimed he'd been only fourteen. *Fourteen!* She couldn't imagine what terrors an adult must deal with seeing the things Bashir had, but he had been a child. He hadn't deserved any of it.

She should have remembered this path would

take them by the slum. She'd been so excited about taking him on a tour of her home, like he had his yacht, that she hadn't thought out their every step beforehand. And now he was glum, and any joy they'd had disappeared.

At least she now understood why he was trying to build his nonprofit. Since he had the ability and wealth to do it, Bashir would help the people who were going through what he had suffered. Rather than allowing the cycle of tragedy to continue, he was putting a stop to it.

"The worst part was the helplessness. I didn't think I'd ever escape."

"But you did," she said, her throat raw with the tears she forced back. She wanted to pull him away from there, but she knew that would do no good. His memories would go wherever he went, and she couldn't change that, but he was wrong; she could add a bit of hope to a bleak reality. Gently, she led him from where they stood, their link solidified by their hands.

When they stopped again it was down a narrow road with long timber-and-brick buildings flanking either side of them.

Before he asked, she said, "It's the market in Katanga." She hadn't turned her back and run from the slum but took him to the pulsating heart of it. "The people here aren't as helpless as you might think. Those who can, do. And so then we can do our part."

Yusra sniffed the air, a smile splitting her face when she recognized the tantalizing aroma. She left Bashir and approached the old man who owned the food stall. When she circled back to him, she handed him one of the two grease-stained newsprint wraps in her hands and was several shillings short, but it was worth what was coming.

"Careful, it's hot," she warned while peeling back the newsprint from her sandwich wrap.

"What is it?"

"A *rolex*." She laughed at the wrinkle in his brow. "It's not the fancy watch you're wearing, but a popular breakfast wrap. It's basically an omelet and vegetables wrapped in chapati bread. Don't worry—you'll like it just as much, if not more."

He took his first bite, blowing to cool the freshly made sandwich before he did.

Bashir's appreciative groan told her every-thing and restored her confidence that she'd done right in bringing him to Katanga, and that as first dates went, this one wasn't a spectacular failure in the end.

That was the best feeling of all.

They were holding hands again.

Bashir noticed it had happened after they finished eating their rolex wraps, the delicious mid-day meal perking him up, but Yusra was bringing his buzz to dangerous limits when she grabbed his hand and interlaced their fingers together once more. This time he didn't think it was because she believed they'd lose each other.

The Katanga settlement was a maze of tight corridors, with people squeezing up against each other in the narrowest of spaces, but it wasn't overly cramped. They had plenty of room between them. And he was far too tall and too broad to blend in anywhere. She could've spotted him several feet away, so he wouldn't fall for the excuse she had used earlier.

Given Bashir had been on pins and needles around Yusra since the start of their date, it wasn't the most intelligent idea for him to entertain the allure of her. He was treading dangerous waters...

Yet here he was, touching her and liking it all too mightily.

It might have helped if the date was bad. But not only had their day gone incredibly well, even the one moment that could have blemished it all was turned around because of her quick thinking. She'd lured him into different stores, giving him reasons to spend money and help out the store owners who were also slum residents. It did his soul good, and Bashir got the feeling that Yusra had known that, and it was why she'd brought him to Katanga after all he'd told her about his life in a refugee camp in Crete.

When they finally emerged from the neighborhood, they immediately backtracked to where they'd left their motorbike. On a high from how nicely their day had passed, Bashir wasn't as averse to riding the blasted vehicle. He didn't even mind the stares he was getting as they whizzed by on the freeway. A large man like him on the back of a bike rather than in the driver's seat. But he acknowledged Yusra was the far better driver. She'd get them home safely to their sons. He hadn't thought he'd miss Zaire and AJ for a few hours, but he did and more greatly than he expected.

Thinking along the same line, Yusra said over her shoulder, "I'd like to go by the market before we head to the hotel. I wanted to grab some things for the fridge, and the boys are running low on healthy snacks." She'd gotten tired of the hotel food and taken over the kitchen in their suite.

This market had a similar vibe to the one in Katanga except for the colorful tented stalls. Yusra called it Owino Market. She shopped for produce, stocking up on everything she needed, and he carried her shopping bags instinctively. More than simple instinct though, it felt natural to do those things for her.

"Let's stop here. AJ likes the oranges from this stall. I hope Zaire does as well." She touched his arm to grab hold of his attention.

Bashir tried not to lean into the sparking imprint her hand had left behind. But like all the other times they came into contact, he was weakened by a blow of lust for her. He was one big throbbing nerve ending. Vulnerable to every little sensory provocation from her.

Like when she turned to him with an orange closely hovering beneath her nose. She sniffed and sighed with a dreamy smile, her eyes fluttering shut. "Mmm! I love the smell of oranges. If I could bathe in their juices, I would."

He wished he didn't have that image in mind, specifically as the vendor of the stall sliced an orange into fours and handed a quarter to Yusra before holding another quarter out to Bashir. The older woman mimed an eating gesture while she did it, smiling broadly and speaking in Swahili to Yusra, no doubt knowing she could translate.

"It's rude to refuse. She'd take it as an offense, and I like the fruit she sells, so you have to taste some. Spare me the embarrassment the next time I come to visit and buy from her," she said in Somali, magnifying the intimacy of the moment. Enhancing it hundredfold when she accepted the quartered orange on his behalf and tiptoed to get it as close to his mouth as she could. She almost reached him too…

But she'll need a hand.

Body on autopilot, and his common sense on pause, Bashir kept his eyes steady and unblinking on her when he gently curled his fingers around her wrist and drew down to meet her. The orange angled just right for his mouth to close over it; he started with a teasing lash of his tongue. Tangy citrus juice shot straight along his tongue to the back of his throat. Nowhere enough of what he wanted though, he dived back in, eagerness egging him on. He wrapped his mouth around the orange itself, her fingers just touching his lips, but held frozen to do his bidding while he helped her feed him. Then he bit down, his gaze blacking out everything *and* everyone but her. Only Yusra existed in that time and space plane. They could be anywhere, and he wouldn't know it with her large, heated eyes locked on him.

She held on to that orange just as tightly as he had a hold of her.

And he wouldn't have stopped them if it weren't for Yusra moving away suddenly.

She blinked, and her eyes widened for a whole new reason. Before she turned her head, he read the embarrassment streaking over her pretty face. And it was that shyness that had her ignoring him while she pointed out the oranges she wanted bagged before she paid the vendor for the service.

Then with no other choice but to engage him, she looked up but right through him and said, "We should get back to the boys. Alcina, as great and experienced as she is, could use a break."

Bashir sucked the orange clean, its outer husk all that remained, and dumped it in a nearby bin. Leisurely licking his lips, and watching her eyes follow the movement before she hurriedly evaded his stare, he nodded. It was more information he slotted away.

Another thing he'd learned about her.

Yusra desired him, and it equaled the attraction he felt for her. But one look and he knew that she wouldn't act on her emotions, not like he had.

Because she's stronger than me.

Shame seeped into him and churned sour the sweet orange she'd given him. It wasn't the note he wanted their first date to end on, but it was the last thing he remembered at the end of the day.

CHAPTER NINE

BASHIR HAD HIT a wall in his marriage with Yusra.

He'd anticipated it would happen eventually.

Just not as soon as it had.

And now that it had occurred, he had no idea what to do or how to overcome it. Because if they didn't, their relationship could be jeopardized.

And what did he do instead? Pretend like nothing was wrong.

Like he wasn't constantly replaying the last time he'd been alone with Yusra over and over in his mind, pausing only when his head pulsed painfully from the strain of remembering each minute detail from their date.

Their one and only date.

Bashir had thought their outing had been going well, and he'd even hoped they would get to do it again and more frequently. But that was before he totally blew that chance out of the water. A muscle twitched near his eye at the memory. His jaws firming together, and a headache thundering closer.

Just thinking of where it had gone wrong for him was enough for him to relive the shamefully awkward moment at the end of their date. Even now he questioned his uncharacteristic actions. Why had he grabbed her when she'd offered him a sun-ripened slice of orange? The feel of her warmth beneath his fingers, of her pulse at her inner wrist under his thumb and his sharp recall of her hitched breath, widened eyes and quivering lips was eternally branded in him.

He didn't think he'd look at an orange the same way ever again.

He had been a man possessed. Obsessed with the need to touch her. Throughout their date the temptation intensified, and naturally he had reached a breaking point.

That's not an excuse.

Self-loathing laced the thought, bitter and hateful.

He shouldn't have done anything to make her uncomfortable. Now he had irrevocably ruined the harmony they'd found in their convenient relationship. And with every day that passed, Bashir felt more certain Yusra wouldn't be able to get over what he'd done to her.

Apologizing had been his first goal. But getting the words out of his mouth was far more of a challenge than he anticipated it would be. Where did he begin? What did he say to her that wouldn't cause her any more discomfort? Bashir had spent so much time mulling over these questions and more that a whole two weeks had passed since the incident. Which only amplified the charged silence between them and heaped on the hopelessness he'd begun to feel about their sensitive predicament.

Still, none of that fully severed this irresistible pull he had to her.

To prove his point, his world screeched to a halt when Yusra stepped into his field of vision.

She exited the masjid, her teal-blue abaya instantly noticeable, her shoes in hand until her bare feet crossed the threshold. Having cleared the mosque, she slipped back into her pyramid-studded sandals. She crouched down before Zaire and AJ, helping them with their shoes. The boys had chosen to go along with her to the women's section of the mosque rather than join him where the men were praying. He hadn't been hurt by their decision. Her strengthening bond with their sons made him all the more certain that Yusra was perfect for their children, which in turn underlined just how terribly he'd bungled things with her.

And how important it is for me to fix it.

Shielding her eyes, she searched for him among the crowded outdoors, spotting him quickly when he stepped out from behind a large family who had umbrellas to shade them from the blazing afternoon sun. Searing rays of light beat over their heads but gave them a pleasing cloudless blue sky to look up at.

In that clement weather, Yusra approached him with their sons. Once they saw him and were close enough within reach, she let AJ and Zaire go, and the toddlers launched themselves at his legs. He hauled them up easily into the air one after another, their peals of laughter no doubt heard throughout the grounds of the mosque. Bashir basked in the happy music of their joy. He hadn't known it could be like this. With Zaire alone he'd felt like the luckiest father—but now that he had AJ too, he wasn't only lucky, he was blessed.

Swinging them up above his head and having their gleeful chortles rain down over him was the height of happiness for him.

He could name only one other thing that was missing.

More like *who* was missing.

Breathless from playing with their sons, Bashir caught Yusra appraising him with a patient smile. She was gorgeous with sunshine showering her, her brown skin glittering and her cheeks rosy from the heat baking off the ground. The urge to embrace her clanged through him loudly.

Of course his second thought wasn't anywhere

near as harmless as longing to hug her. His gaze roamed her figure. Her abaya couldn't conceal her curves from him, not when he'd felt the swell of her breasts and hips against him before. He looked to her mouth, his own lips sparking in answer...

No, damn it!

Bashir jerked his head away from her. What was wrong with him?

Angry at himself, he would have stormed off and gotten distance from her, but this wasn't the time or place to do it.

They were in the courtyard or *sahn* of the Uganda National Mosque on a Friday afternoon. Not shockingly, the masjid buzzed with energy. People were filtering out of midday prayer, Jummah, on the holiest of days for Muslims, and so, much like a church-on-Sunday mass, the congregation had a larger turnout than on any other day of the week.

When Yusra had asked him to join her and the children for the afternoon service, Bashir couldn't refuse. It had been a long while since he'd prayed with family.

Nostalgia, sweet and bitter, came to him in waves. Emotions he had long buried and even forgotten, and not all entirely sad, ebbed and flowed like the ocean tides. His mother's long robes in one hand, his father's rough palm gripping his other and the cheerful chatter of his brothers and sisters and grandparents as they walked out of a Jummah prayer together.

Bashir slowly but surely saw the faces of his long-lost family members more clearly than he had before today, and he owed it to Yusra. Without her he wouldn't have considered bringing Zaire to this sacred place. And it was one more reason why he shouldn't act mindlessly around her.

Pushing her away was a risk he couldn't take.

She was good for the children. Good with him. Somehow, some way, he had to heal what he'd broken.

And soon.

Even if it meant they had to revisit the topic of intimacy in their marriage. After all, it was either that or...

I create more distance between us.

Bashir didn't know which was the right choice, only that he'd had enough distance from her already, and he was tired of it.

Talking Bashir into climbing the minaret's three-hundred-plus steps to the top wasn't as hard-won a battle as Yusra imagined it would be. He had simply nodded, assenting when she pointed up to the masjid's abutting tower and asked, "Could we stop to take a look at the view from there?" No argument or questions asked.

And she wouldn't have minded his automatic compliance, if he weren't acting like a zombie again.

It had started right after their first—and last—date.

Yusra flushed hot all over just thinking about it. She'd have sworn Bashir branded her wrist from when he'd grasped her and used her to feed himself the orange slice she had offered him. He'd certainly left a searing imprint of the moment in her mind for possibly the rest of her life.

And she still didn't know whether that was a bad thing or not.

She rubbed her wrist, catching herself in the midst of the absentminded action. Blushing anew, she refocused her sights on the unbeatable views of her adopted city, and hoped by the time she peeked Bashir's way he was no longer staring at her broodingly.

"Isn't it breathtaking?" she exclaimed. "They call it a skyscraper mosque."

Bashir carried Zaire, while she had AJ in her arms. They walked the whole balcony, the three-sixty vista as shockingly high as she remembered, before she stopped and regarded him with what she hoped was less embarrassment written across her face.

"You know it's our one-month anniversary tomorrow."

"I didn't," he said in an unusually gruff tone, his eyes darting away from her down the steep drop to the masjid's courtyard below. The people looked like dots from up here. Not that she was paying anything else any mind, not with the way Bashir was acting.

Did he not care about that milestone?

Their relationship might not have been brought about by love, but it was still a marriage. And she could still celebrate having lasted together for a whole month.

"I thought we could do something to commemorate it tonight. Dinner maybe?"

"Maybe," he said, again his tone decidedly blasé. Like none of it mattered to him.

Like I don't matter.

She couldn't stop feeling the way she did. Though she didn't have a right to it. She was his wife, yes, but theirs was a convenient partnership. They equally benefited from having married each other.

But I still care.

She stiffened her lightly trembling lower lip and popped up her chin, fighting back the frustration that burned through her and rivaled the sun's heat. It wouldn't do her any good to allow Bashir to get under her skin. To permit him to be any closer to her. This was as far as they should go, as a couple on paper but never in practice.

"Before we go to your ship, I'll need to stop by the office." As per their agreement, and just as they'd done every week for the last month, they were moving to his colossal yacht for the weekend. "There's a couple things I have to grab for work."

Bashir jerked his head in the briefest of nods.

Skin flushed now and sweat misting her brow, she glared at him. Surely the heat of a thousand suns couldn't feel hotter, yet he remained annoyingly cool in the face of her glower, and even looked away from her with a stubborn wrinkle to his brow.

What was wrong with him? Was he just being deliberately cruel, or was it something she'd said or done to offend him?

She couldn't even laugh when Zaire reached a tiny hand out to Bashir's long, curly beard and brushed at his father hesitantly.

Her first clue that something was wrong was the sudden weakness in her limbs. She'd believed it had been fatigue from climbing the stairs and hauling AJ up as well, but her muscles quaked and her heartbeat sounded in her ears. Her stomach clenched incessantly, reminding her she'd skipped breakfast.

"What's the matter?" Bashir demanded.

So, he'd noticed something was wrong with her. His turn in mood might have left her with whiplash if she weren't busy trying to fight to control the world from swimming out of focus. Yusra closed her eyes and leaned against him when his arm circled around her, lending her the support she hadn't asked for but needed in that moment.

"Juice box," she said weakly, opening her eyes and patting her purse.

Bashir swept AJ out of her arms, which gave her a chance to search her purse for the sugar boost. It took two boxes, and some time recuperating against the wall of the tower, to regain her senses.

The first thing she could see was Bashir's barely restrained irritation.

"Did you not have anything to eat this morning?" he asked sharply.

She smiled nervously, fatigued from the low blood sugar. "I didn't have as much time for breakfast before we left the hotel."

All she'd had was a granola bar and a banana after she had taken her insulin. She blamed sleeping in, which wouldn't have happened if she hadn't stayed up late to work after she'd tried and failed to go to sleep. And Bashir was partly culpable for that. Yusra had kept herself awake thinking about why he was being so strange around her.

Was it really only because of the incident with the orange?

Or is this who he really is? Distant. Detached. Unreachable.

Everything she didn't want in a life partner again.

Swiping her tongue over dry lips, she said, "It's fine. *I'll* be fine."

"Still. You should have told me."

She didn't see how that would make a difference. *And why is this more important than our marriage?*

Her face must have communicated that petulant thought if Bashir's downturned mouth was any indication.

"We'll stop by your office *after* we grab something to eat." His tone brooked no room for negotiation.

She wouldn't have argued anyway. Her traitorous stomach chose that moment to grumble loudly, revealing she didn't mind his suggestion at all.

Seeing no resistance from her, he asked, "Can you walk back down the stairs?"

Was that concern she heard in his voice? *For me?*

Feeling silly about getting happy over something as benign as Bashir checking in on her, Yusra said, "I think I can handle it."

"If you can't, you'll tell me."

That was definitely concern she heard. *Inter-*

esting. For someone who'd walked around for two weeks like she hadn't existed, barely acknowledging her unless there seemed no other way around it, he appeared to have suddenly reverted back to who he'd been on their holiday-slash-honeymoon and, more recently, their date.

Though it didn't explain why Bashir had been like a completely different person with her lately. Of course she could ask him directly. But for that Yusra would require a full stomach and all her wits about her.

CHAPTER TEN

"WE SHOULD TALK."

Yusra's mouth popped open when Bashir uttered the exact same words as her at the exact same time and with the exact same urgent inflection.

If she needed a sign that the universe was thrusting them in this direction, she had it.

"Not here. Follow me," he ordered once his shocked expression wore off.

"Okay," she said squeakily.

Bashir's tall, hulking figure stalked ahead of her through his yacht. She hurried to keep up with his long strides, not wanting to fall behind. Getting lost on his large mazelike ship was a strong probability for her. An embarrassing admission as she'd now stayed a few weekends with him and should have known one end of the yacht from the other.

Her legs ached and cramped slightly when they finally stopped.

Yusra marveled at the salon he'd brought her to. Her eyes immediately landing on the room's central feature.

"Is that the *ocean*?"

"It is," Bashir replied.

She gawked at the glass wall, her feet in their slippers itching to go closer to the bruised black-and-blue waters shimmering under an array of dimmed LED lights attached to the ship's outer hull. Yusra wouldn't have expected to see anything like it on Bashir's yacht. Not when she knew that he didn't have the warmest relationship with large bodies of water. And yet he'd managed to surprise her, and that in and of itself wasn't a shock.

Her husband had proven he was a man of many layers.

Almost as greatly as she wished to touch her hand to that glass wall and *feel* like she was grasping the whole of the ocean in her palm, she wanted to peel back Bashir's layers to find the heart of him.

And then maybe I'll feel like I truly know him. Truly trust him.

As it was, she was still hesitant around him, especially given how he'd been acting, and so she calmed herself by glancing around the lounge area he had shown her. Painted and furnished in muted tones of beige and gray, and with its darkly varnished hardwood flooring, the salon oozed untouchable wealth. Skylights brightened her path to where Bashir stood and watched her from the middle of the room, his arms stiffly hanging at his sides, his hands clenched into fists and his shoulders subtly raised higher.

Great.

His defensive stance wasn't easing her mind. Like a bottle of fizzy soda shaken up, her belly roiled with her bubbling anxiety. Maybe she'd have been better off not indulging in the princely dinner that Bashir had asked his chefs to prepare specially for their one-month wedding anniversary. As lip-smacking good as the meal had been, the food wasn't digesting nearly as well as it had tasted.

But she couldn't run away from this anymore. She had to talk to Bashir tonight and right then. And it felt fated now that she knew he'd been thinking the same as her.

I just have to speak my truth. Easy.

That encouraging thought in mind, Yusra placed her hands over her upset stomach, willed courage to her, and walked as close to him as she could without running into his big strong chest.

Staring down at her without flinching was impossible.

Bashir ground his teeth against the rise of cowardice. None of what he'd done as of late felt like him. His actions, like his words, were an antithesis to what he *actually* wished to do.

I want to hold her. Kiss her. Give her pleasure like she'll never know with any other man.

"Bashir? Did you want to speak first, or should I?"

He nodded briskly. As gracious as she might think the gesture, the truth was he couldn't get a word out right then, not with his teeth locked together as crushingly as they were. If this kept up, he'd need a crowbar to pry his steely jaws apart.

"I'll come out and say it then. You've been acting really weird, and I can't help thinking it's because of me."

Her knitted eyebrows, large, sad eyes and downturned mouth could have doubled as a dagger plunging into his heart. His fists balled so tightly that the tendons of his wrists sent flaring pain signals to his brain, all of which went ignored. All that his mind turned over was the discovery that he'd hurt her.

I didn't mean to...

Bashir hadn't even considered that she'd have flagged the change in him. But now it was so clear to him that she would. It hadn't been the first time Yusra had intuited his mood before. She'd done it in the waters of the Nile where they had swum together, and he had ended up sharing the story of his treacherous *tahriib* by sea.

And she had done it again now.

"Are you angry with me?"

"No." He spoke with more force than he intended, and he withered inside when Yusra startled back from him.

Bashir's hands moved on their own. Grasped her wrists and pulled her in as he stepped closer to catch her against him. She came willingly, no fight registering in her, even as she gawped up at him. Only this time none of the fear he'd seen spark through her eyes was present. Shocked confusion snuffed it all out. *Good.* This was far better of a sight. And what a sight she made in his arms, her softer, smaller figure flush against his taller, harder-cut body. He didn't know how it had come to this. All he'd been thinking was that he hated this distance that had come between them. And his body acted on his deeply seated emotion.

Bashir waited on the regret for touching her like this again to barge its way through and bring him to his knees. Counted the seconds until she was ripped from him by his own cowardly thoughts and feelings.

One. Two.

He didn't get to three because he heard himself rasp, "I'm far from upset with you."

Then as though he wasn't a split second away from beating his chest and proclaiming her as his woman, he pushed air out through his nose, channeled civility and continued.

"I'm angry with myself, and I'd understand if you were too. Back in the market, on our date, I shouldn't have touched you the way I did. The way I am now." He regarded where her hands were splayed on his chest, caged there by him. "It's why I propose we reopen discussion on the parameters of physical intimacy within our relationship."

"O-okay," she stammered up at him.

"I was aware before we married that you showed lack of interest in being intimate, and since marriage we haven't shared a bed. Can I safely presume then that you're still not interested?"

"I'm not ready to share a bed, no," she spoke quietly, her eyes zipping over his face.

He struggled to control the disappointment surging in him. But her decision had to be unaffected by how he felt. He wouldn't have her any other way. If Yusra wasn't interested, then he could learn to grow uninterested too. And it was why when she asked, "Do you feel differently?" Bashir said no, even though he did and to such an extent he no longer recognized himself.

He then gazed at her with the heated depth and breadth of yearning he'd sealed away over the past couple weeks.

One last time, he vowed silently, committing every detail of them together like this to last him through their marriage. *Forever*.

Before Bashir broke his contact with her and began what would surely be a tediously long path to celibacy, he caught Yusra's lips tilting up into a smile. Her laughter came precious seconds later.

Bewilderment shot through Bashir's face, his brows storming down over his narrowed eyes, his soft, full mouth pinched at the corners, lips pressed firmly together.

Yusra could understand why he was confused.

To him it had to have looked like she was laughing at him—she wasn't—but she could see how he might think that.

"I'm sorry!" she gasped at the end of the giggling fit. "It's just that *I* thought you were upset with me when *you* were thinking the same about me." Widening her eyes, she hastily said, "I swear I'm not laughing at you."

He gave a snort and a small chuckle.

She giggled again. "It's funny, isn't it? And all we had to do to save us all this time and grief was talk to each other like we just did."

Bashir's brooding confusion thawed quickly after that. His gusty laughter rolled up into hers, their mirth making the most beautiful of symphonies. Yusra had a feeling she'd be a wealthy woman herself if she uncovered how to bottle and sell their happy sounds.

At the end of it, she pushed her hands against

him, her laughter gone but her awareness of him stronger. There was the quiet power of his long thick fingers on her wrists, the hard unyielding heat of his body, and the reverent caress of his eyes on her.

"About the market that day, with the orange, I never told you how I felt."

At her words, the storm cloud that darkened his face returned. Full of crackling thunder and gloomy rain, it drowned their happiness.

As sad as her heart was, she held her ground, knowing they needed to leap over this hurdle before they could get back to where they had just been. She was doing this because she wished for the laughter and easy conversation with him again. There was still so much she didn't know about him, and they weren't going to get over this but *through* this, together.

"There's a reason I haven't said anything." She wet her lips, her heart in her throat and drumming wildly at her ears simultaneously. "Truthfully, I liked it. And knowing what we said about physical intimacy, I didn't want to upset the new balance we've found after the honeymoon…er…holiday."

"Honeymoon," he corrected roughly, his dark brown eyes brighter, his thumb gently massaging the inside of her wrist. His touch provoked a shiver up and out from her core and a wash of goose bumps over her skin.

She fought to clear her mind and continue what she had to tell him. "After our *honeymoon*, I wanted everything to be as perfect as it was. I wouldn't have let an orange ruin it."

Stroking her, he said in a rough voice, "It was a damn good orange though. If anything would have ruined it, it might have been that."

"I told you that fruit stand sold the best oranges..." She trailed into a sigh when he freed one of her hands and gripped her hip instead. If only she wasn't thwarted by all the clothing she wore. A thermal long-sleeved shirt, drawstring joggers and a fleece robe kept her toasty when she had been wandering the yacht's chilly passageways in search of Bashir before he'd found her instead. Now her clothes were obstructing her. She quivered at the thought of having his lightly calloused fingers and big warm palm on her naked flesh.

Another shiver rocked through her when Bashir slowly lifted her hand to his mouth, her fingers treated to a delicate kiss from him. One by one, his mouth alighted on each of her digits. With her free hand she dragged her nails over him to form a fist.

A switch flipped in her mind and the last of her fight evaporated. Even her fear in placing complete faith in him faded and, for once, gave her peace of mind in its absence. And it was a peace she deserved because Bashir had yet to give her a plausible cause to distrust him. It was how she knew she wasn't going to pull away from him. *Not this time.*

"Stop me," he gruffly commanded.

"I won't." Yusra defied him. Nothing and no one would rob her of what she knew was coming.

Bashir's narrowed eyes roved her face, and like the kiss he slowly, methodically pressed to the center of her palm, she felt it all over her body. Her breasts were heavy from her need of him, her thighs crushing over the source of relentless, driving heat between her legs.

"If you don't stop this now..."

His warning trailed off sharply, his breath hitching when she sprung up on her toes and kissed him. Well, kissed his beard, because she couldn't climb higher on her own.

Bashir freed a mixture of a grunt and moan. "Yusra." He dragged her name out, his shoulders bunching and flexing, his hands tightening over the parts of her he touched and his eyes locked on her mouth. "Do you want me to kiss you?"

Yes!

But all she could do was nod and pant eagerly. Nothing she said anyway could encapsulate what she was feeling.

Nothing except when he hauled her up so suddenly against him, Yusra experienced weightlessness. She was suspended by a fusion of her desire for Bashir and her trust in him to care for and please her. And the only thing that eclipsed the feel-good head rush of being dipped back by him and lovingly held close to his body was his mouth inches from her own. His hot breath mingled with hers and then, blissfully, he was there, exactly where she'd envisioned him all along.

It was a kiss to end all the other kisses she'd had before.

With that kiss, she forgot her jerk of an ex-husband, forgot her anxieties around the institution of marriage, and thanks to Bashir, she didn't even recognize herself.

Like who had that wanton moan come from? Who was clinging on to his hard, broad shoulders, and arching her back to get him to follow her and deepen their kiss? Who nipped his full and very soft lower lip when he didn't give her what she wanted?

Finally, Bashir groaned and gave in. Tipping her backward, he upset the *shayla* off her head, the slinky shawl slipping down to her shoulders before sliding to the floor. He broke their kiss, murmured, "Sorry," and might have said more if she didn't lock lips with him again.

The kiss left her breathless and wanting, her thighs chafing each other in their quest to have Bashir wrapped around her legs. Wrapped in her. As if he heard her thoughts, he fulfilled her fantasy, lifted her up and pinned her to the cool glass wall framing the ocean he dreaded. And never once did he stop kissing her, stop delving into her mouth and stoking a fire in her body and soul that rose higher, *ever* higher, until she was certain she'd combust from the overload of pleasure.

Still, she wouldn't tire of this. Not ever.

It was a shame they required air, their pathetic lungs begging for a breather. But it didn't stop her from clinging on to him, her hands sliding to the back of his thick neck and holding him to her desperately. She didn't want to part from him. Not even when dizziness dimmed her vision and swooped over her limbs. Her legs quaked under her, and if Bashir weren't supporting her, she'd have gone limp on the floor. She closed her eyes as her husband pulled away from her, his breath cool against her wet, throbbing mouth, his husky voice akin to velvet on her sensitized skin as he asked, "Are you all right? Is it your blood sugar?"

Opening her eyes, Yusra gazed at him smilingly while panting. Even looking sexily rumpled and ready to kiss the life out of her again, he possessed a rarefied self-control. She didn't fault him for being able to compartmentalize his emotions. Because she had witnessed his passion, and it had been solely and intensely directed at her.

"It's your fault. Kissing me to death." She laughed, rested her head on his steady chest and sighed dreamily. "It wouldn't be a bad way to go though."

"You're not going anywhere," he said as he swooped her wobbling legs out from under her and carried her, "but here, on this sofa, where you'll rest until you can stand on your own two feet."

Ever the gentleman, Bashir went back to retrieve her *shayla* from where it had fallen. Then he sat with her on the sectional sofa and positioned her legs onto his lap. Those small actions from him warmed her almost as much as his sweet, sexy kisses had done.

For a while they simply stared at each other. The silence pleasant and interspersed with their labored breathing.

She could have said a million things to him when her breathing evened and she could speak clearly. And she settled on pointing to the salon's glass wall and asking, "So, why this view? I presumed you disliked large bodies of water."

"I fear the ocean, that's true, and yet I appreciate that it's a home for many creatures. Then there's its beauty and life-giving qualities."

Under Bashir's potent gaze, Yusra could have mistaken herself for the ocean he lovingly described.

It was a mistake she happily didn't correct in her mind.

CHAPTER ELEVEN

BASHIR'S KISSES HAD been the reset they needed.

And in the days that followed, Yusra felt a certainty in their marriage working out. It might have just been positive thinking on her part, but whatever it was, it reflected in other parts of her life too. Business had picked up for her, and she had graphic design projects scheduled an entire year ahead. And with that, her bank account wasn't looking so anemic anymore. She'd finally let her apartment go after giving the pushy landlord all of his back rent. Leaving her neighbor Dembe was difficult, but they hadn't been seeing much of each other since Bashir came into her life. She'd also paid off what she owed on her office space to the laundromat owner before packing up and setting up her new workspace in their hotel suite. With his tuition paid for, AJ was back in day care, and Zaire had joined him when the boys refused to be separated for even a few hours. And after all that, Yusra had enough left over for her copays on her insulin and diabetic supplies.

She had not one but several reasons to be optimistic.

The best part was she'd started her art again.

That was how Yusra found herself sitting across from her old college friend Samira in her friend's well-established art gallery.

"When I got the call from you, I couldn't believe it. I haven't seen you in so long," Samira said, hugging her again before they walked through the substantial gallery and climbed the floating staircase to the offices on the second floor.

Where Yusra had married and ultimately walked away from the art they both loved, Samira had gone on to interning with a well-heeled auction house. From there she had worked her way up the ladder before branching off and opening her own gallery to showcase artists. Yusra would be lying if she denied her envy. But her happiness for her friend's success won over.

"I can't believe you really did it. Opened your own gallery." It was all Samira had talked about when they'd been starry-eyed art majors. "This place is *big*. I know you have to be reeling in artists left, right and center."

Her friend smirked, giving away that she was, indeed, flush with choices when it came to picking which artists to lift up into the limelight. But rather than give her the lowdown on her business, Samira pushed Yusra down into the club chair across from her in the warmly lit, stylishly furnished office and she gushed, "So, is that a ring I see on your finger?"

"It's a long story, but yes," Yusra said with a blush as she covered her brilliant wedding bands with a hand, her thoughts careening over to Bashir. Like she hadn't thought of him on and off every day already. The man claimed prime property in her mind, sometimes even pushing out the things that should've mattered like, now that they had kissed, what came next?

More kisses…

Or just *more*.

She didn't know. But seeing that Samira wouldn't listen without hearing this story first, Yusra gave her friend what she clearly wanted, all the juicy gossip without the kernel of truth that was her marriage of convenience with Bashir.

So it felt disingenuous when at the end Samira sighed happily for her.

"Good. You deserve a second chance after that no-good dirtbag of a first husband."

Samira had known Yusra's ex, Guled, and she hadn't liked him, not then and certainly not now. She had warned Yusra about him, and she'd been right, but that was the past. No point in tearing open old wounds.

"Tell me about this Bashir. Does he love you? Do *you* love him?"

Yusra was saved from having to respond by a doorbell chiming somewhere in the building.

"I thought the gallery was closed for the setup of the new exhibit," Yusra began to say. She had seen a glimpse of the exhibition coming together below, the theme of reclaimed African art captured perfectly in an assortment of mediums by Samira's chosen African artists.

Samira popped up off of her chair and smoothed her hands down her trendy burnished-yellow pantsuit. "It is formally, but that would be the back door. I have a delivery."

Left alone while her friend conducted her business, Yusra wrung her hands and recalled her morning with Bashir. She had confessed to her anxiety about visiting Samira and asking for a chance to showcase her art. It would be a big ask. Samira wasn't an up-and-coming novice gallery owner. She had trotted the continent and even gone as far as Europe to see the best that the art world had to offer.

"What if I'm not good enough?" Yusra had fretted. *She'd pushed at her plate—her breakfast tasteless to her in the face of her fears. "I don't*

want her doing this because we're friends. I want it only if she believes I'm good at what I do."

He'd held up a hand. "Stop. See, right there. That's your problem. You're worried about what she'll think of your art."

Bashir had stood and walked to where she sat. Cupping her trembling chin, and then framing his big hand over her cheek, he'd said, "You do your art for you, always. Nothing will stop you then, not even your fears."

Yusra had smiled silly at his confidence in her. It was so alien and yet refreshing to her to have a partner who supported her. Thinking of Bashir again, she toyed with her wedding rings absentmindedly and drifted off. From somewhere nearby she heard the muffled sound of voices followed by heavy footfalls closing in on where she waited for her friend to return. Could Samira have come up with the delivery person?

Yusra didn't have time to prepare. She sat, eyes wide, caught twisting her rings when the door to Samira's office opened and Bashir walked in with Samira trailing behind him.

Before she could ask why he was there, he apologized and explained, "Sorry to intrude. I have time-sensitive news, and I thought it was better that I deliver it in person rather than over the phone."

"I guess one of us still has a delivery." Samira

winked and prompted Yusra's face to heat with a blush. "I'll give you some privacy," her friend offered kindly and turned to make herself scarce.

But Bashir stopped her from leaving.

"Actually, Yusra and I will walk your gallery."

"Sure, I could stretch my legs," Yusra agreed, masking her apprehension at what her husband had to tell her. What news had brought him out to see her? Whatever it was, it had to be big. She knew he wouldn't have disrupted her meeting otherwise.

As he led her away from Samira and down to the gallery floor, Yusra prayed that whatever he had to say wouldn't add to her frayed nerves.

"Greece?"

Yusra grew still beside him and her head spun from the elephant sculpture of colorful flip-flops they had been admiring, to stare up at him.

Bashir handed her his phone, figuring he would articulate himself better with images. She looked through aerial black-and-white photos of his nonprofit's construction site.

"I have drones sending back photos daily." Since he couldn't be present in Crete where Project Halcyone was being built, he had used his plentiful resources to bring the project to wherever he was. And lately that had been by Yusra's side, either in her city or on his ship. He hadn't wanted that to change, but she had been adamant once not to leave Uganda, so he would respect her wishes whatever they were.

"But *Greece*?" She sounded unsold.

"Yes, Greece. It would be until construction on Halcyone is completed. Another six weeks are projected. And if you're amenable to the idea, we'd reside at my home in a small village on the island of Zákynthos."

She shook her head, murmuring, "I need to think this over," and walked around him. With him following her, they continued to weave through the art gallery her friend owned, the art itself a blur to him now that his focus was on her.

"Of course, since I'm dropping this on you suddenly, it would be understandable if you didn't agree. The other option would be that I go to Greece on my own and the children remain with you here in Uganda." It wasn't an option he even wished to consider. Being apart from Zaire and AJ would be torment enough. But gazing longingly at Yusra, Bashir accepted he'd also miss his vivacious wife. Things had changed for the better between them, and they had regained a harmonious balance and peace in their unconventional marriage.

And it's all because we kissed.

Bashir passed his hand over his smiling mouth. Unleashing his pent-up lust for her and receiving an enthusiastic response in return had been apparently just the cure they needed to mend the rift in their relationship. And that was why this was a difficult decision. He didn't want her to come along and be unhappy with him in Greece, and he hated to leave her and worry that he was jeopardizing their marriage once again.

He was damned in either scenario.

"You'd really leave Zaire with me?" she asked, bringing them to a halt before a mixed media artwork of a slumbering baby in a traditional kitenge swaddle, not unlike the ones he'd seen women using to carry their young children on their backs around the city. Though parts of the painting were rendered in oil, the child's swaddle appeared to be crafted with threads of silk, cotton and some other soft cloth. It homed in on the exhibition's theme.

Tearing his gaze from the painting to her, he nodded. "He won't like being separated from you and AJ, and I trust you'll care for him."

"That's sweet of you, but won't you miss the boys?"

"I'll adjust, and it won't be for long," he lied. Six weeks was a long while to be apart from them. But to ease her mind, and his own, he said, "I can also fly home for the weekends."

Home?

The strange sensation that came with that realization quickly passed and what remained was a surety that Yusra and their sons *were* his home. But that didn't help him commit to leaving them behind. Even knowing it would be a temporary separation, it felt like his heart would burst from the misery.

Yusra touched a hand to his chest, her eyes probing him, and she appeared to have found what she was looking for when a sadness alighted over her. "All of that sounds well-thought-out, but it's not what you want, is it?"

In the reflection of her dark eyes Bashir saw himself, the stress written on his face not as cleverly hidden as he'd have liked.

She pressed her other hand to him, her neck craned back for him, a kind smile pulling at her round rosy-brown cheeks.

"Don't sacrifice your happiness for ours."

"I'm…" He was about to tell her he wasn't, but that would be another lie. And she'd already seen through his first one. Sighing wearily, he said, "All right. I'm not happy."

"Do you want us to come with you?"

His brows rose higher. Was that a trick question? If it was, he didn't care, he honestly replied, "Yes."

Her bright smile told him he'd answered correctly even before she spoke.

"Then we'll go with you."

"Just like that?" he asked, tempering his excitement in case he misunderstood her.

But it was obvious he hadn't when she took his hands in hers. "This means a lot to you, and I want to be supportive like you were when I told you about revisiting the artist in me."

He had done that, but because he'd selfishly loved seeing the luminosity in her eyes amplify whenever she spoke of her precious art. So, naturally, it had become precious to him too.

"You won't regret coming with me?"

"I promise there will be no regrets." A grin shaped the mouth Bashir had been fantasizing about more since they'd kissed last—this morning, but that had been three hours ago, and he was overdue another taste of her.

"Six weeks might be too long," he argued half-heartedly, the other half of his heart dead set on her joining him.

"Bashir, stop. I want to come with you, and the boys will miss you too. We either all go, or none of us do."

Hearing those words put to bed the last of his doubts that she was doing this out of respect for him rather than truly desiring to remain by his side. And now that he wasn't tangled in his negativity, Bashir's elation broke free and soared. It compelled him to hug Yusra to him. Crush her close until he couldn't discern where she started and he ended. She laughed against his chest—happy, fluted notes that captured his feelings perfectly. If they could remain like that all day, he'd see to it, but the approach of clacking heels on the laminate flooring forewarned their private moment had reached its end.

Yusra's friend Samira beamed at them, a phone clutched in her hands.

"I don't mean to interrupt, but I was ordering lunch and I didn't know whether to order for two or three."

"I'm not staying," Bashir told her.

Samira nodded and walked a short distance away to complete the lunch order for her and Yusra.

"Have you proposed your idea to your friend yet?"

Yusra pressed her lips together and shook her head. She went from being relaxed in his arms to having tension thunder across her face. Her idea wasn't a bad one. Bashir had glimpsed her art in her office, and she possessed ample talent. She just needed a confidence boost.

"Repeat what you told me at the dining table. Show her that passion and you won't fail," he advised.

She nodded meekly.

"Then again, I could bribe your friend by buying artwork…"

That had the desired reaction. Any sign of her uneasiness disappeared as Yusra swatted his chest lightly and cackled in mock horror. "You wouldn't."

"I would if it was what you wanted or needed, and it's neither of those because you're a born artist and this place is crying out to showcase your heart and soul. So, go. Do your friend a favor and don't deprive her of your calling."

Yusra sniffed and blinked fast. Her eyes shinier after what he said. She pressed her heated cheek back to his chest and hugged him quietly and far more fiercely. He read her gratitude clearly. No words required.

"We'll talk more about Greece tonight, but I'll let you get back to your lunch date." He dropped a kiss on her forehead before he talked himself out of the tenderhearted gesture.

Letting her go was hard, but it had to happen. At least he had gotten to see her.

At first in an effort to not disturb her, Bashir had wanted to relay his news to her over the phone. But he was glad he hadn't. Seeing Yusra in person had been the brightest spot in his busy day.

And perhaps it was his ego running the show, but he wondered if that was true for her too.

Was seeing me the best part of her day?

Bashir discovered he sincerely hoped so.

CHAPTER TWELVE

BEFORE HE'D EVER entertained the notion of having a family, Bashir had lived alone most of the year in his isolated Grecian villa.

Out of the eight homes he owned throughout the world, these sprawling acres of undulating green valley interspersed with golden beaches and unobstructed views of the blue-as-the-sky Ionian Sea was hands-down his favorite. And he didn't share that opinion alone.

On her third day of her temporary stay in Greece, Yusra jabbed her spoon teasingly at him over her bowl of Ugandan millet porridge and said, "You thought that six weeks was too long, but I think you'll have more trouble getting me to leave this place."

And that encompassed his mood exactly.

Never had he believed he'd have missed living there, particularly as his last memory of being in idyllic Zákynthos wasn't as rosy as its scenery. Getting the call from a hospital in Uganda and learning of his cousin's death had happened on

this island paradise. That had been a dark day,
and just one more to toss onto the pile he stored
in his memory. Others included the day he'd lost
his family to a flash flood, and then again when
he had nearly died in the sea on his cross-conti-
nental journey to Europe.

Bashir had been fully expecting to experience
some upsetting flashbacks when they'd first arrived in Zákynthos. And he had, but his memories were murky and soft-edged, the brushes
of disquiet against his mind gentler than he remembered. Certain spots of the villa itself were
packed with more memories than other areas. His
bedroom for one had been where he had kicked
out of his bedsheets upon receiving the distress-
ing news that Imran had died. The entrance hall
was where he had dropped his car keys twice in
his hurry to drive himself to his private airstrip.
And the pristine white gravel up the driveway
would always remind him of the grinding sound
of his tires as he raced from his home to fly to
Uganda, where he would eventually meet and
gain custody of Zaire.

No, coming home wasn't what he expected.
But that isn't a bad thing.
It helped that Yusra and their boys were enchanted by the island. Its varied sandy beaches,
craggy cliffsides, turquoise sea and charming
village life were all things his wife and children

experienced and delighted in just the last few days alone. And despite his workload Bashir joined them on all their family outings. He hadn't wanted to miss the expressions on their faces for every little new thing they did.

Today was no different.

After playing with Zaire and AJ at the secluded beach connected to his vast property via a private trail, the boys fatigued themselves into longer than usual naps, and Bashir proposed he and Yusra take a stroll of their own through the village closest to their home.

Her enthusiasm doubled when she saw his preferred mode of transportation. A gleaming blue high-end sports convertible, the roof down promising swift, sea-laced breezes on their faces.

"It's not your *boda boda*, but it's all I have to offer."

"It's perfect, Bashir!"

He grinned widely and was as close to preening as he'd allow himself. "It's yours soon—your international driver's permit is in the mail." He had plenty of other luxury vehicles at his disposal. Besides, the delight on Yusra's face was worth every euro to his name. In the face of all the things he owned, his ability to make her and their sons happy was priceless. Bashir shut the door on the other emotions swirling in there, not ready to analyze what his growing affection for her meant for their future, and whether he should be concerned by any of it.

They were living in the present; that was all that mattered.

And right at that moment they had an impromptu second date to go on.

Perfectly timed, Yusra turned to him and said, "Let's make this a date to remember," right before they roared out of the villa's long drive, the car engine purring smoothly as they accelerated onto the serpentine road with its sublime views. The fertile valleys on one side and on the other end a plunging limestone cliff with no barrier and the spread of aquamarine sea. And yet even then, with everything else to look at, his eyes were always drawn back to her.

She eventually caught him in the act, a slow-forming sexy smirk playing over her sheer-glossed lips when she had him.

That, right there, already made this a date to remember for him.

For so long Yusra had looked forward to another outing with Bashir, and now that it was happening at last, she spent it walking on eggshells and keeping an eye out for warning signs that the date was taking a bad turn.

She didn't want a repeat of how things ended on their first date together.

Didn't wish for anything to go wrong when everything and everyone was being so achingly perfect.

Every person they met welcomed them warmly. Some even stopped to strike up a chat with Bashir, their conversation friendly enough for Yusra to glean that her husband had friends on the island he called home once.

Which added to the mystery of why he'd left picturesque Zákynthos.

What had taken him from this paradise on earth? It was true that she no longer viewed his ship as being a cold and colorless attempt at what a home should be. Rather than seeing it as a floating prison that her powerfully wealthy husband used to separate himself from the world and the hazards it sometimes possessed, Yusra saw it as a place of refuge for him in the eye of the storm.

And now it's mine too.

That ship connected them, just as much as their marriage did. It had been where Bashir had proposed to her the first time. And it was where their family lived whenever they weren't on dry land.

But her newfound appreciation for his superyacht didn't settle her curiosity of why he'd chosen anywhere else but this island to raise a family.

She had mulled it over quietly through their stroll of the village grounds, and then again over their authentic Grecian lunch of garlicky baked eggplant, or *skordostoumbi*. But she had her limits, and she reached a breaking point where she couldn't hold her nosiness in any longer.

"Why did you leave?"

Bashir didn't miss a stride, his gait easy and relaxed, deceptively so because he studiously kept his eyes from meeting hers.

"Would you believe me if I said the island life had grown to bore me?"

She gave a snort. "I've done my research, Bashir. This place is known to host some wild parties, and tons of tourists tend to flock to this locale during the summer. Between those two you'd have a hard time finding nothing to do, and no one to talk to."

His laughter, deep and gravelly, fired a blush from her and the sweetest relief. For a second there she believed she might have pushed his buttons a bit too far. As curious as she was, she still wanted their date to go smoothly. She could push him, but only so far.

"The truth of why I left is simple in a way, and complicated in others." Looking at her directly, he then asked on a foreboding note, "Do you still want to know?"

Beneath his heavy-lidded gaze, she nodded slowly, her anxiety compounding on itself. Was she opening a box of ills that was better left undisturbed? She didn't know, but it seemed too late to back out on her decision now.

"I left because I was home here on the island when I learned that Zaire's mother died and he needed me. As you might have guessed, it wasn't the best of situations, and it left an ineradicable memory of this place."

"I'm sorry. I shouldn't have asked."

"Don't be. I thought I'd feel that way for the rest of my life, but I was wrong. Coming back here feels different but…good. Better than I imagined it would anyway."

Even if he was just saying that to make her feel less awful than she did about her nosiness, it was considerate of him to say so. And maybe that was why she disregarded the nagging sensation that Bashir hadn't been entirely forthcoming with her and there was more to the story than he had let on.

That feeling persisted in her until they returned to his car and drove a short distance away from the village's center. The road he took was rougher and narrower, but it passed directly through rows of olive groves. During their lunch Bashir had explained that the olive oil used in their meal came directly from local olive farms. She licked her lips whenever remembering the oil's perfectly warmed, richly fruity taste.

Bashir drove as fast as the locals did on the

country roads, the ease with which he knew this island's terrain speaking volumes. Again, Yusra found her mind wandering to why she sensed that he hadn't been completely truthful of his reasoning to abandon Zákynthos for almost three years.

But why would that be?

And what could he be hiding if he was lying?

This time it was more of a challenge to dispel her rising doubts.

Distraction came in the form of Bashir turning into a long gated drive. He shifted the gear of his car to climb the inclining road, and with time Yusra glimpsed where they were headed. Buildings dotted the landscape of the valley, and the stone-built structures formed a concentric circle around a taller, three-story white stone edifice.

Bashir parked at the entrance to this central building.

"'Imran Villas and Suites,'" she read from the gold-lettered sign once she stepped outside the car.

Bashir circled over to where she stood, his head tipped back like hers, his sunglasses shielding his eyes, but his tone clearly proud when he said, "This is the first resort that I've owned, managed and renovated from the ground up all by myself."

She'd almost forgotten that he was a successful hotelier. He didn't speak of his job often, but it was plain to her that he loved what he did, and that passion had made him a billionaire tycoon. And now that she knew what this place was, Yusra marveled at what he'd created, pride ping-ponging through her a heartbeat later. "Can I see it?"

She didn't miss his quickly flashing grin.

"I've already booked us a tour of one of the villas. We'll even have time to stop by the closest olive farm. The family who owns it has been in business for over two hundred years, and they've promised us an experience and taste of their olives like no other."

More delicious olives? That sounded great to her.

Yusra packed away any apprehension over what Bashir wasn't telling her, and she slipped her arm around his. He looked down at where she held him abruptly. But he didn't shrug her off, and once his surprise melted, he curled his biceps around her arm in return.

They walked the grounds and entered one of the villas.

Yusra sucked in a brisk intake of air at the beauty of the indoor-outdoor space. The first thing she noticed was the long, moving wall of glass. Bashir pushed a button on a small remote and the walls began folding in on themselves silently and their absence let in cool, sea-scented air. She tipped her face to the breeze and sighed her pleasure.

Wandering deeper inside to get her fill of this one-of-a-kind space, she felt Bashir's presence near her. But he didn't hover. Or prohibit her from touching anything. Instead, giving her the space to poke around the cavernous part concrete, part stone villa, he lingered close enough if she needed him, but far enough to let her curiosity guide her.

It took her a while to tour the building's interior, but she did at last make it outside. Because that was where she had wanted to go right from the start. How could she resist the inviting waters of the infinity pool, stone-paved terrace with its alfresco dining space and the wooden sun lounger shaded beneath a canopy?

She walked around all of it; her awe must have been written all over her face because Bashir came up next to her.

"If you like it so much, we could spend the night. Alcina won't mind caring for the boys for a while longer." They'd left his trustworthy nanny with AJ and Zaire before leaving their home.

But as tempting as his suggestion was, more for the reason that she would have time alone and uninterrupted with him than taking a break from the endless energy of their toddlers, Yusra couldn't take him up on the offer.

Shaking her head, she said, "We shouldn't, at least not now."

"Rain check then."

"Definitely," she concurred.

Gazing out toward the sea, Yusra closed her eyes, and let out another pleasure-filled sigh when Bashir moved her back to his front. The embrace from behind in this romantic spot had her questioning whether she'd been hasty in declining to stay here with him. They had pushed the envelope a little more every day since having kissed, and as nice as that was, Yusra was tiring of their slow, teasing pace. Like foreplay with no end, it only ever had her burning up with this febrile longing to be fulfilled by him.

Though she worried if she pushed him too far, he would stop altogether.

And she couldn't have that happening.

Never.

The possessive thought slashed through her mind before her consciousness blanked when Bashir's hands moved on her. He explored her cautiously, his big hands sliding up from her waist over her softly rounded stomach beneath her flowing long-sleeved tunic, and across the buttons that kept her shirt in place.

Far slower than she liked, he brushed his fingertips over the buttons, one by one, rising higher until he reached her shirt's collar. He unfastened the topmost buttons, careful not to bare her completely except to his searching hand. Bashir's thick fingers reached inside her shirt and rubbed across her clavicle before he dipped his digits teasingly to the valley of her breasts. He did this beneath the cover of her tunic, but anyone who could have happened on them would know, just by the placement of his hand, and the way her head tossed back against his chest and she moaned breathily, that he caressed the top of her heaving chest.

Yusra gasped, "Lower," and arched up into his seeking hand when he listened and another of her buttons was freed. He cupped her breast with one of his large palms, his warmth seeping through her cotton bra to singe her flesh.

I just need him a bit closer...

And lower. Much, much lower.

Unexpectedly Bashir's hand stilled both under her shirt and against her hip. Then, after a torturous pause, he completely pulled back from her without explanation.

At least not at first. Because then she saw for herself what had compelled him to stop.

A familiar-looking older man stood waveringly on the threshold of the villa's interior and exterior areas.

Yusra didn't look closer immediately to figure out where she'd seen this man before. Rather she shielded herself until she had her appearance in order. And by then Bashir crossed over to the man and ushered him indoors, giving her additional time to fan her heated face and calm her jittery emotions.

When she felt as presentable as she could be, she walked over to where the two men were now chatting with ease. As she neared them, Yusra recognized where she'd seen the older man.

At our wedding!

He was Bashir's mentor and friend. The one who had hugged him so fiercely.

Otis. She recalled his name.

Now Otis beamed at her, his friendly smile easing her embarrassment of having been caught with Bashir where they had been seconds away from a more compromising position. But she tried not to think too much on that.

"*Kalimera.* Hello again. Yusra, is it? Enchanted to meet you!" His boisterous, happy voice rang through the villa. It made her smile more brightly.

Taking her hand, Otis gave it a kiss. "I'm sorry that I didn't get a chance to formally meet you at your lovely wedding."

"It's all right. We're meeting now."

Otis laughed gustily. "That's true! My wife and I are visiting the island, and we stopped by your home first, but we were told you both weren't home."

"Well, you found us easily enough," Bashir drawled.

Yusra snapped her head up to him, surprised to hear a gruffness in his voice. It was borderline rude.

She compensated for his shocking rudeness with a shining smile. "We're sorry you missed us. Bashir was just eager to show me his villas and hotel suites. And I was just as eager to see them."

"Ah, of course! Perfectly understandable! This one's a favorite among his other establishments."

"Is it?" Yusra swung her gaze to her dour-faced husband before she agreed, "But, yes, it really is a special place."

"As special as its namesake," Otis said.

Yusra's smile faded. "Its namesake?"

She didn't miss Bashir spearing a glare at his business mentor and saying something to him in Greek. She wouldn't have been able to understand anything, but unlike Bashir, Otis's emotions flitted openly across his face, and she didn't need a translator to decipher that. First there was the shock rounding his eyes and drawing his mouth open, and then came the confusion as his bushy, frost-white eyebrows lowered.

Otis acted oddly after that, his jovial expression reading as less genuine to her, as if something was bothering her. She could only make an educated supposition that it had to do with whatever Bashir said to him in Greek. And whatever it was that transpired in that other language steered Otis toward the villa's exit. With a nervous-sounding laugh, the older man called back, "Bashir, I'll be waiting over at Reception in the main building. *Endáxi*." Then to her he waved awkwardly and said, "*Adio* for now, my dear."

Otis's departure introduced a weighty silence.

A silence Yusra ended when she asked, "For now?"

"Otis and his wife, Evgenia wish to stay with us while they vacation for a few days."

Yusra didn't see a problem with that. Their home was huge, and the chances of any of them feeling cramped were slim. So she was baffled by why he looked as though that living situation wouldn't be feasible.

"Bashir, they'll stay with us."

He grunted noncommittally, but his brooding frown said otherwise.

She could've asked him what was bothering him—because something clearly was, but instead she blurted, "What did he mean that this villa has a namesake?"

If Bashir had appeared perturbed before, there was no denying his blatant troubled expression at her question. Quickly though, he shuttered the emotions filtering onto his face. And she could have stamped her foot out of frustration in just the same way their toddler sons did whenever they were throwing a tantrum.

She felt cheated. Like Bashir was showing her the parts he approved rather than the whole messy palette that made up who he was. And she wanted all of him: not bits and pieces, but everything that was her broodingly beautiful husband.

Yusra opened her mouth to convey her riled-up thoughts and feelings into words, but Bashir slammed an iron door shut on the conversation.

"I should go to him. I'll call a cab to take you home."

She hurried after him, catching him at the door with a hand on his back and a gasped, "Wait!"

"What?" he sighed, his gruff exasperation wounding her already aching heart. He glanced down at her over his shoulder, as if giving her anything more might be too much for him right then.

But why?

Why is he acting like this?

Yusra's mind reeled. She didn't want to say the mean things that came to her through her pain. Later, she knew, she'd regret all of it. So, she did what he wanted. She withdrew her hand and silently gave him permission to leave.

Not that he needed it. Bashir stalked away from the villa's entrance without another look back. Watching her powerful husband retreating from her was not the way she'd pictured their day ending.

Yusra had hoped this date would be their do-over. But now...

Now I have to wonder if we aren't cursed.

Or maybe it wasn't that they were cursed at all, but plain old incompatible with each other.

And that caused her far more torment than if they were just unlucky.

CHAPTER THIRTEEN

HOSTING BASHIR'S SPECIAL guests might have been pleasant if Yusra weren't stuck in her own head. But she was, and it was ruining what could have been a lovely dinner with new houseguests. And as much as she wanted to place the fault on Bashir, she couldn't. He hadn't forced her to trust him. Nor was he to blame that she began to care for him so deeply that her despondency only magnified as the day went by and the silence between them stretched on.

When Bashir had finally arrived home, he had come with Otis and the two men headed straight for the darkly furnished study that Yusra viewed as the perfect man cave. Bashir hadn't even bothered to make eye contact with her. Meanwhile Otis had paused long enough to greet his wife, Evgenia with a hug and a kiss.

Yusra hadn't known jealousy as fierce as hers in that moment, and it greatly disturbed her.

It was right then that she knew she had to keep herself preoccupied. Bashir had a personal chef, but Yusra had relieved her in the kitchen and sent her home early. Slaving over the hot stove was all that kept her from crying over this impasse with Bashir.

Well, that and playing with Zaire and AJ when they awoke from their nap, which gratefully had been by the time she came home alone and sulking from her and Bashir's failed date. But eventually she left the boys with Alcina and Evgenia while she prepared dinner. And while she was in the kitchen, she gained a semblance of power.

Cooking was like art to her, just with different ingredients than when she was working with her charcoals, oil paints and pencils. Yusra was in her element, so nothing should have gone wrong. But she wasn't wholly herself, and so after she heard robust laughter and Bashir's name called out, she swiveled her head in that direction as she was pouring hot water into a pot of caramelizing onions…and burned her hand.

She cried out and dropped the pot.

No one came in to check on her. She was cut off from everyone else, so she came to her own aid, running her fingers through cold water. Yusra sniffled as she located the first aid kit, applied salve and wrapped her injured hand. She worked more cautiously after that, but the damage was done. Her fingers throbbed painfully. But compared to her crushed spirits, it was nothing. Her hand would heal; she knew that. She wished she were as confident about her trust being restored.

Once knocked down by her ex-husband, and now shaken up by Bashir, that outlook wasn't so bright.

Dinner with their guests was full of lively conversation. None of which Yusra contributed to or paid any heed. By that point she had fully retreated into her mind, shut the door and waited for her duties as hostess to end.

For his part Bashir wasn't the most gracious of hosts either.

He grumbled plenty during dinner, glowered at his food for more than half of the time, and generally brooded his way through to dessert which was served in the family room. Yusra skipped on the crème caramel dessert she'd made for their dinner party. Usually, the dessert would remind her of home, her mother's baking and the wonderful warmth guests could bring with them, but all she felt was a coldness driving into her skin, through her bones and into her bloodstream. Her brain felt frozen; her heart along with it.

Together she and Bashir must have made for a miserable duo.

Lucky for them, his friends were good people. An affable couple, Otis and Evgenia carried the conversation all on their own at times, regaling them with tales of how they'd met through an arranged marriage by their powerfully wealthy families. They hadn't felt love for each other at first, but rather admiration for their passions— Otis in hotel management, and Evgenia as an interior designer.

It wasn't unlike her and Bashir.

A marriage of convenience arranged by them to solve the issue of the baby swap wasn't very different than an arranged marriage, was it?

And Otis and Evgenia grew to love each other.

Yusra stared at the older couple with hope whenever they looked to each other, their love glowing undoubtedly in their eyes.

But unlike Otis and Evgenia who had been open to love, she and Bashir never were.

It was why they'd ultimately married.

And it's why I'm unhappy. She startlingly accepted the epiphanic thought. *I love Bashir.*

What a foolish thing to do. Falling for a man who, although her husband, was the last person she should love. Now what was she going to do?

Knowing what he had to do and doing it were not only two very separate things, but one was harder than the other, and Bashir discovered that personally when he found himself pacing the length of his bedroom. He needed to see and speak with Yusra, but he couldn't bring himself to go to his wife. His extremely lovely wife who he was realizing he wasn't treating right.

I don't deserve her.

But that wasn't his only problem.

He liked her. Immensely. So much, in fact, it struck him that somewhere between meeting her and kissing her he had fallen in love with Yusra. And no matter how good that love made him feel, it was transient. Like life, love was fleeting. He loved her today, but what if tomorrow stole that love from him? Even today didn't promise a guarantee.

Bashir regarded the old photos of his family strewn on his bed, some faded and yellowed and others as clear as the day the photos were taken. But they were all proof of his point that love wasn't everlasting.

He'd loved his cousin, Imran, and he had thought leaving him would stop him from caring. But then his cousin died, and the heartache he was running from only caught up with him in time.

Would it be like that if I lost Yusra?

If she left him one way or another, would he ever recover from that loss?

No, the answer came to him instantly. He wouldn't be the same. Losing her would wreck him, more now that he acknowledged that what he'd been feeling for her this whole time was love. Deep and true romantic love.

Bashir slowed to a standstill, hating that he

had to do what came next. But he couldn't hide out in his room all night. After a tense dinner only saved by Otis and Evgenia's cheerful humor, he'd shown his old friends to their guest room before retiring to his own bedroom. Of course it was then he had recognized that he and Yusra shouldn't sleep apart for the short duration of their houseguests' stay. What would Otis and Evgenia think if they learned of their marriage of convenience? Knowing them as he did, they'd ask questions of him, and pry in that annoyingly loving way of theirs. And that wasn't something Bashir wished to handle on top of everything else on his to-do list.

But it was a good excuse to go to Yusra. From there he would nudge them toward what he needed to tell her.

Striding to his door, Bashir flung it open and stopped in his tracks.

Yusra stood in his path, her hand in the air, knuckles ready to rap on his door, and a warm-looking woolen blanket curled to her chest. She lowered her hand slowly, looking shy all of a sudden, almost queasily so as she shuffled her feet.

He stepped aside with a silent invitation.

Once she was in his bedroom, he closed the door.

"I thought I should be here with you. I didn't want your guests to wonder why we were sleeping in separate rooms." She turned to face him, her shyness still mingling with obvious discomfort. He didn't like to see her like that, hated that he was likely the cause. Bashir surmised he had to be after the way their day had gone.

Now that he *knew* he loved her, it was through that lens that he looked at her.

But he had to shatter that lens. That was his goal.

Because I can't love her.

The risk to him was too great.

"I was just about to go say the same thing to you," he said.

She hugged her blanket closer. "So, are we both taking the bed? I could sleep on the sofa." She pointed to the love seat across from the king-size four-poster bed and before an electric fireplace. Between the two of them, the sofa would be a better fit for her than him, but Bashir wouldn't have it.

"No, you have the bed."

"Are you sure?" She glanced cursorily at it. "It's big enough to fit us comfortably. I wouldn't mind…"

You will after what I have to say.

Bashir shook his head. "The bed is yours, Yusra. I'll be fine wherever I sleep." He could fix a makeshift mattress out of extra blankets if he needed to, but he wouldn't have her sleeping roughly on his watch.

Nodding, she quietly went to place her blanket atop his bed, and right after, she appeared distracted suddenly. He saw why when she picked up the photos he'd forgotten he had left out in the open.

"Is this your family?" she asked.

Too late to prevent her from seeing them, he supposed it was a smooth enough segue to what he had to tell her.

"Yes, that's them."

The photo she held was one he'd committed to memory. It was his only picture of his family. Everything else having been washed away with the flash flood that killed them. If it weren't for his aunt finding the photo in an album, he wouldn't have been able to recall the faces of his parents, grandparents and siblings.

"It's all that I have left of them. It was our last Eid together as a family."

"And this one?" She held up a photo of his aunt and uncle.

"My aunt and uncle. They took me in after my family died and I had no one else to care for me."

There was only one photo that remained after that. Bashir tensed his muscles in preparation for when Yusra lifted up that photo to him. He'd thought he was ready, but he wasn't, and so it showed in his gravelly voice.

"That's me…and my cousin Imran." In one of the last photos with Imran before Bashir had run away from the only other family he had. And he wasn't counting Yusra and their boys, even though he should because if this conversation went south, he might lose them too. Forcing that despairing thought away, he said, "Imran was my favorite of all my cousins. We were close. Almost like brothers."

"Imran. Is he the one the villas and suites you showed me today are named after?"

Clever of her to connect those dots. But he'd seen her working it out the instant Otis had let drop about the resort villas having a namesake.

"That's correct. I dedicated it to him." But that had been before Imran died. Now the name held even more significance to Bashir.

"You look happy," she said and stared at the photo of his smiling self. In that photo, he had his arm looped around his cousin, and even though Imran had been older by a few years, Bashir had been a few inches taller and so comically his cousin stretched to get his arm around Bashir's shoulders.

Like the other photos, he'd gazed at that picture of him and Imran so many times, he had every detail trapped in his mind.

"We were happy," he finally said, his fists at his sides, jaws clenched achingly tight. That was it. He couldn't put it off any longer. And he wouldn't find a better window of opportunity when she looked up and her eyebrows bunched together.

"What's the matter?" she whispered.

"There's a reason I was looking at those photos, and a reason I'm telling you about my cousin." An awful beat of silence, and then, he said, "He was AJ's father."

"AJ's father…" she murmured, shook her head in disbelief and looked at the photo in her hand before her eyes snapped up to him once more. "If he's AJ's father, that means… You lied."

"I never lied. I just didn't tell you about Imran."

"Why?" she cried, controlling her voice so that it never rose above a harsh whisper. She dropped the photo and marched over to him. "Why not just trust me and tell the truth? What happened to us communicating openly?"

"I didn't think it was a big deal," he lied.

"How can you say that when he's AJ's father!"

"*I* am AJ's father."

"That's not what I meant and you know that, so don't twist my words, Bashir. Don't you dare," she hissed warningly, her finger stabbing the air between them, and though she didn't touch him, he felt her angry jab all the same. Right over his wildly thumping heart. Prompting him to rub his chest.

"You're making this a bigger deal than it truly is." It was an incendiary comment. He knew it, and that was why he said it.

And sure enough Yusra froze up and stared at him, openmouthed, her eyes full of confusion like she didn't even recognize who he was.

Bashir wanted this. Her fury and his.

For the majority of their relationship, everything had gone so perfectly, it always felt like the other shoe would drop at any moment. Now that it had with his omission of truth, reality could set in. And if he was extra lucky it would diminish his love for her.

But it wasn't meant to be.

Because right before him her anger eroded, and in a shocking twist, she asked with a tremble to her chin, "Why are you doing this?"

"Telling you the truth, you mean," he said gruffly.

"Being an ass, I mean."

Her colorful language was another surprise. And with each one, he was losing grip on his plan to kill his love for her.

"Okay, I get it," she said on a shaky sigh, her head bowing, but her brokenhearted voice rising up. "Maybe you didn't trust me enough to know how I would react. And I never said you weren't AJ's father. Both Zaire and AJ are lucky to have you in their lives. I see that. And I'm not negating what you mean to our children. But you continued to lie about your cousin. Which means you still don't trust me. You can't imagine how much that hurts—"

She broke off, sniffled loudly and spun away from him.

Though not quick enough for him to miss the wetness on her cheeks.

She's crying because of me.

At that Bashir bit the inside of his cheek so hard he tasted blood, and with it an incessant pain where he purposefully wounded himself to feel anything else besides a guilt so vast it could rival the span of the sea near their home. But it did him no good.

With each tremble of her shoulders and soft sob from her, Bashir felt the worst of the worst.

She hid her wet eyes, her back to him as she spoke tearfully. "I guess now's a poor time to tell you that I love you." Then she turned around and swiped at her face, what little good it did her.

More tears rained down, replacing what she wiped clear and dripping off the chin she proudly thrust higher. "Did you hear what I said?"

"Clearly," he gritted.

"And?" she challenged.

He knew what she was after. A reciprocation of love from him. And he would have given it to her if he wasn't who he was, and if his past had been any different than what it ended up being.

But it isn't.

"And I don't feel the same."

She dropped her head, her sniffles making a comeback.

"I can't love you, or anyone else for that matter. Yusra, I didn't run away to Europe because I wanted a better life. I ran away from the only other family I'd known because I was scared to love them and lose them just like I had my first family. And I left Imran behind because I thought I was doing the best thing for me, but I lost him anyways, and it still hurt like hell. I won't do it all over again."

He hoped that was enough to open her eyes on choosing her love wisely when it came to him. He was no good for her.

But Yusra lifted her head and gazed so forlornly at him that it nearly had him buckling under the pressure of having hurt her. "My ex-husband never shared his thoughts or feelings, and he left me out of his life. I've lived like that once already. And like you, I won't do it all over again. Because right now I don't have faith in you, and that… That's just as important as love is to me.

"I love you, Bashir, and that's why I can't do this."

She turned then, walked to the en suite and locked herself inside.

Bashir chased her to the closed door, where he raised his hand to knock and call her back out. But he stopped himself and forced his feet to go the opposite direction. Away from the bathroom Yusra claimed as refuge from him, away from his bedroom where he prayed she slept well after their fight and away from his home with her and their sons.

If there was ever a time for him to return to his ship, now was it.

CHAPTER FOURTEEN

YUSRA COUNTED THOSE first days that passed by the growing collection of finished artworks piling up in her bedroom. She obsessively created art. Not stopping even when she ran out of space. Simply, she used spare rooms all over the villa to store her pieces.

By the end of that first week without her husband, she finally found a dedicated workspace in Bashir's study. And since the owner of this palatial villa wasn't home, she did what she pleased.

Serves him right.

Yusra painted a hard, bold stroke over the new canvas, her broken heart guiding this latest piece. She used darker colors and the overall mood was ghastlier when she completed it hours later. Black, red and green swirled together in a chilling eddy and best captured the three emotions that had been her default for a week now. Outrage, envy, and worst of all, a desolation that wouldn't quit.

She was angry because he'd left her when they should have been trying to work it out together.

Envious that he clearly wasn't as affected as she was. How else could he continue to work on his precious nonprofit like everything was normal?

But the sadness with no end was the worst of all three.

Even after she'd cried all the tears humanly possible, she couldn't dislodge the lump in her throat or rub the itchiness from her eyes whenever she recalled her last moment with Bashir. She sobbed herself to sleep and stared off into space whenever she wasn't doing her art or caring for AJ and Zaire.

Without the boys she'd have probably curled up in bed all day, and with only her misery as her constant companion.

But they gave her a reason to get up and get on with her life. And if Bashir could act as though nothing transformative happened in their relationship, then so could she.

And he did eventually call, asking her how she and the boys were faring in that irritatingly calm, even tone of his: the very same tone he'd once used to tell her about the baby swap that had changed their lives. She let him speak with their children, but it was only ever that. She ripped a page out of his book and channeled a dispassionate version of herself.

That was how the next month passed. In this

state of disconnect between her emotions and thoughts and her body. She cared for AJ and Zaire, worked on the several graphic design projects her clients expected from her by their deadlines and created the art she'd been yearning to make for years now.

Yusra didn't think she'd ever want to feel again.

Then at the end of the fifth week, she realized two things. One, Bashir's nonprofit, Project Halcyone, would be opening its door in a short while, and secondly, she had cut herself off from her emotions but her love for her husband hadn't gone anywhere.

She still loved him.

More than that…

I miss him.

And just as she was accepting that fact, a gift arrived with Bashir's aide Nadim.

After making his delivery in person, Nadim left, no doubt returning to his employer who cowardly hid out on his ship, and Yusra carried Bashir's mystery gift box away from where their curious toddlers could tear into it and break whatever was inside. She opened the box a while later when she found the time to be alone.

She gasped as soon as she saw what it was.

Paintbrushes. And not just any paintbrushes, but an entire set of Winsor & Newton Series 7 Kolinksy Sable Brushes. The whole set had to have cost hundreds—*thousands* if she gave her best estimate. And, yes, it might be a drop in the bucket to Bashir, but it meant the world to her. These brushes were reserved for the serious-minded artist. And somehow, he'd thought she deserved them.

Yusra didn't realize she was crying until pattering footsteps discovered her in the study amidst her art. Zaire came first, closely followed by AJ who was clutching their pet rabbit to his chest. Three sets of eyes peered at her. Two tiny humans and a cute, fluffy bunny. All three equally mystified.

She pulled them in for a hug, squeezing them close and laughing when Zaire touched one wet cheek, and AJ the other.

Yusra kissed their small hands.

How could she tell them that she was thrilled with their father? That for the first time since their argument more than a month ago, she was in a buoyant mood. Seeing the brushes was the first step in a positive direction.

Just holding them between her thumb and index finger and posing a brush's tip in the air awakened a long-slumbering inspiration in her.

I should do something for him. To show him I'm not mad. That I still love him.

Because it was so clear to her now.

Bashir was scared. He didn't want to lose her;

he said so himself in as direct a way as possible. He'd lost his family before, twice over, and naturally he worried. That still made him a coward, yes. But he was *her* coward.

The father of her children.

Her husband.

Her love.

One of the last things she'd said to him was that trust and love were equally important to her. And she still stood by that, but now that she wasn't looking at the situation through an angrily sad filter, Yusra had faith in one thing: that they would lose each other and their family if she sat here and did nothing.

But what can I do to show him that I love him?

She looked down and found the answer was in her hands all along.

And she had the perfect muses in mind.

With that, Yusra gathered her boys—and their adorable rabbit—closer and she cheerfully asked, "Who wants to help Mommy make a painting?"

CHAPTER FIFTEEN

"EVERYTHING IS IN PLACE, including the extra event you added to the schedule, and we're almost ready to begin with the auction."

Bashir turned to acknowledge Nadim's report with a cursory glance, his eyes veering back from his trusty aide with his equally trusty tablet to the ballroom. They were up on the stage that was temporarily erected for the special night. From that vantage point he could see everyone filing into the grand space they had arranged for their esteemed guests. And that was perfect because he had no plan to miss her when she arrived.

Yusra.

He had called to confirm whether she was coming. And though she gave him a hopeful answer, he still erred on the side of disappointment. Lowering his expectation would protect him if she didn't show up. Of course, like the sucker that he was, Bashir still hoped she would.

He missed her terribly. So much in fact that he

was starting to feel physical effects of it. Headaches being the worst of it.

"These should help," Nadim said as he passed over a bottle of painkillers discreetly.

Bashir headed for the back of the stage, hurriedly dry-swallowed the pill and walked back out to keep a watch for Yusra. He wouldn't miss her.

"Have you spoken to Alcina? Did she mention whether they're en route?"

"Not yet," Nadim told him. "But the reporter arrived a short while ago. Security let him pass and they're keeping an eye on him as you've requested."

Bashir scowled. It wasn't the news he wished to hear. The reporter from the business journal had interviewed him once already, and it had nearly been a train wreck when the man had gone off the preapproved list of questions and entered more sensitive territory with Bashir. He abhorred doing it again, but when the journal called and asked for a follow-up interview at his charity gala and auction, Bashir couldn't refuse. Not when he could see the sound mindedness of having a reporter on hand at such a pivotal event for Project Halcyone. As long as he kept the questioning period short and on topic, he'd fare better than he had last time. If the reporter wanted juicy details, he'd get them, but he would accept whatever Bashir willingly fed him. No more, and no less.

"The auction will begin shortly. I'll touch base when we're ready for it." Nadim walked away from him, leaving Bashir to be on the lookout for his wife on his own. He just hoped he wouldn't overlook her as the sizable hall grew more and more populated.

Guests streamed in steadily, the ballroom filling up quickly enough. Tomorrow, that same space would be repurposed to house temporary shelter facilities for refugees, asylum seekers and migrants alike. But for tonight, it would cater to the wealthy and powerful elite of all of Europe and not just Greece. Bashir had pulled every string he could and called in favors to promote the interest of the nonprofit. Without funding, Halcyone was nothing. Even with his billions, he could only do so much. So, he hoped his guests tonight were extra generous and opened their checkbooks to the auction he'd planned.

Everything was exactly as it should be. From the magnificent chandeliers hanging down from between blood-red velvet ceiling drapes, to the golden glow those chandeliers cast in the room, their fulgent lights reflecting off the smooth hardwood flooring. Floor-to-ceiling windows showcased a view of the Cretan Sea. A new moon turned the waters an inky black, but inside, the warming sound of string music and growing hum of voices from his guests blasted away the darkest that night could challenge him with.

He didn't have the luxury of standing around and moping over whether Yusra would show in support for him, or if he'd pushed her away too far. A small blessing in disguise. He climbed down from the stage to hobnob with his guests, ensure that he knew their names and that they believed he was the right man to trust their money with when it came time to donate.

An hour into circling the room and making necessary rounds to introduce himself to as many people as possible, Bashir finally had time to himself. He grabbed a *soumada* from one of the drink servers. The sweet, syrupy drink wasn't his favorite, but it was a staple in Crete, and he needed the sugary boost to lift his sunken spirits.

He just didn't get it.

I have my Halcyone finally.

He should have been happier that the dream he'd had all these months was now very much real.

I should be over the moon.

Instead, he might as well have been anchored deep in the Cretan Sea. Sipping at his tooth-achingly sweet drink, he recalled what he'd last said to Yusra. That he couldn't love her. That he was incapable of it. And then he had fled from her, his cowardice bringing him to his ship where for

the past six weeks he hid from her and the love he
had for her that stubbornly wouldn't leave him.

Now he wondered what she was doing. And
whether she missed him at all.

Was she happy that he'd invited her to the cel-
ebration? Or was she girding herself to do battle
and break his heart by asking for the divorce that
hovered over them since their argument?

Gulping more of the *soumada* than he intended, Bashir pressed a hand to his forehead
and squeezed his eyes shut against the spike in
his blood sugar. He felt a presence and squinted
to address whoever it was.

Alcina stood before him.

He looked around her, not smothering his eagerness and not caring that he was being obvious.
"Where is she? Have the boys come with her?"

Alcina avoided his eyes. A clue that he wouldn't
like what she had to report. "They're on their way,
but Yusra sent me along first."

Well. That wasn't the worst bit of news.

At least he now knew she was coming. But before he could question Alcina about how Yusra's
mood had seemed to her, he heard his name.

Otis and Evgenia made their way over to him,
their smiles as warm as the hugs and kisses on
the cheeks he received from both in a custom-
ary Greek greeting. The last time he'd seen either was after he left the villa on the night he had

argued with Yusra. He'd skulked off like a thief in the night, and though he was sure Yusra had tried to save face the morning after, Otis and Evgenia knew him too well. They might not know what had transpired exactly, but shortly after, they had called to grill him on what happened.

And that was when the whole truth tumbled out of him. Bashir told them about the baby swap and the marriage of convenience. He even made it clear that though he loved Yusra more than his life, he was afraid to let her in and lose her.

Much like they had done when they had taken him away from the refugee camp and welcomed him into their home and family, Otis and Evgenia consoled him and passed no judgment. They lifted him up, and it was with their help, and that of Nadim and Alcina, that he was able to be standing where he was now.

"Remember, you have a lot of groveling to do, son. A happy wife guarantees a happy life," Otis warned and wagged a finger at him.

Evgenia hushed him laughingly. "Otis, stop. They know what's good for them, and so they'll figure it out together. Besides, we had the birds-and-bees talk already when he was a young man. He needs none of our coddling in that department. Do you, Bashir?"

Blushing, he passed a hand over his heated face

and shook his head. Bashir was saved from further public embarrassment when Nadim found him.

"The auction is nearly ready to start, but I wanted to let you know that Yusra has arrived."

Bashir's heart juddered. "Where?"

Nadim looked uncomfortable, and he took a few seconds too long to say, "She's speaking with the reporter. Our security team tried to intervene—"

Bashir had heard enough.

He shot off to rescue his wife. Only to discover that she needed no shining knight in armor charging to save her.

Yusra looked glorious in a showstopping, modest gown. The sparkling black of the dress like stars had been plucked and sewn onto the bodice, full-length arms and skirt. She'd styled her black hijab to seamlessly tuck under the gown's high collar. And the alluringly bold black henna twining her fingers popped out to him where she held AJ's and Zaire's hands.

Like a professional, she answered the reporter's queries poignantly at times and more reservedly during others. She even wrenched a laugh out of the reporter at one point. Bashir watched from the sidelines with other guests who began to circle and swarm out of sheer curiosity. He could see why. A woman with two young children made for quite a sight when no one else had brought their children along. He had delivered an explicit rule against younger guests attending, mostly as he wanted the message focused on Halcyone and the funds required to do the good he hoped the organization would bring to the disenfranchised newcomers to this part of the world.

But his children and wife were an exception. Sue him for being a billionaire who broke rules.

All of the questions asked of Yusra revolved around her relationship with him. Where had she met him? How long had they dated? What was married life like with a billionaire?

He hadn't thought she'd noticed him in the crowd, but Yusra's eyes found him suddenly; her beautiful smile felt personal. She kept flicking looks at him throughout the interview, and soon enough the reporter noticed and picked him out of the throng of people. He waved Bashir over to join his lovely wife.

From there they talked about his plans for the nonprofit, and Bashir spoke eloquently and at comfortable length on his hopes for what Project Halcyone would come to mean to those who needed its services.

And this was where he gave those juicy details that he once was resistant to speak on.

"As you know, I was a refugee myself. I came to this country and continent from a distant land. When I arrived, I had no family, no friends, no prospects on what I planned to do for a living.

Twenty years later, I have several resorts to my name, friends who stand by and support me, and a family," he looked down at Yusra, and she smiled and nodded her encouragement, "who love me and who I love very deeply."

Satisfied with that response, and the others he gave, the reporter positioned them for photographs.

While Bashir held Yusra to his side and their boys stood before them, wriggling under the flashing lights of the camera, he whispered, "I'm sorry."

And she said back, "I am too."

It was all they managed before Nadim interrupted just as the interview wrapped up.

"We need you on stage. The auction."

Yes, of course, the auction.

How had I possibly forgotten?

Bashir curbed the sarcastic thought when he felt Zaire and AJ hugging his legs. Just as much as he'd missed his wife, he'd missed his boys. Crouching down to them, he squeezed each of them back, and even let them stroke his longer beard as they liked to do.

Above him, he heard Yusra tell them, "Okay, boys, we have to let Daddy go. He's got work to do. We'll see him later."

Like the moon tempering the ocean's tides, his gaze was pulled up to her naturally. God, he wanted to kiss her. Take her in his arms and remind himself what she tasted like and how it had felt to hold her against him. But most of all he wanted to do as Otis advised: grovel until she took him back.

Until she understood that he loved her.

That he had already experienced what losing her felt like and he never wanted that feeling to return and haunt him ever again.

"I'll be back," he vowed to her. Pulling away felt like leaving a piece of him behind with her, to protect until he returned.

Up on the stage, Bashir found Yusra immediately. She was seated closer to the stage, their children, Alcina, Nadim, Otis and Evgenia at their table. He noticed the seat beside her was vacant, and his heart soared with the realization she'd left it open for him.

The auction consisted of various items from different suppliers. There were rare decorative vessels carbon-dating back to the time of ancient Greece. Artful mosaics from the time of Roman rule in Greece. And even a worn pair of leather sandals that purportedly belonged to the herald of the gods, Hermes himself. Laughable, but they sold well when they hit the auction block.

Yusra's friend Samira had also sent along some of her African artists' works to be auctioned to buyers tonight. And they were a surprise hit with the guests. The auction itself went by fast. The audience gave generously. One by one, each auctioned piece was sold to a new owner. Believing that they'd reached the end, Bashir was surprised when Nadim signaled from backstage that there was one more. An eleventh-hour entry according to the update he was given on the final auction item.

Explaining that the art piece was a portrait of hope from an artist who didn't know its subjects but knew that they had been a great part of the reason Halcyone was built, Bashir grew as mystified as the audience.

Hushed whispers of intrigue drifted up to him as the item was wheeled up.

With a nod from him, the attendants pulled off the covering to a collective gasp from everyone. Or at least that was what he heard, but he couldn't be certain with his ears ringing as much as they were.

He blinked several times and gawked at the familiarity of the scene. It was his family staring back at him from atop one of the many green cliff valleys of his home in Zákynthos. There were his mother and father, his grandparents, brothers and sisters. But others were with them. Imran and Tara. His cousin and cousin's wife stood very naturally in the portrait as if they had really posed for the artist.

Staring at Nadim's tablet, he could see there wasn't a note of who the artist was.

But he had one guess who it could be.

He needn't have searched for her; having mem-
orized where she was seated, his eyes landed
on her easily. Yusra. It had to be her. He had
glimpsed her art, but he hadn't thought she could
bring his long-gone family back to life for him.
And he suspected she'd used the photos he had
shown her as inspiration.

Coughing to clear his throat of the suspicious
thickness of emotion that settled there, he adjusted
his headset mic and addressed the audience.

"I'll open the bid with one million."

Now there was no denying the collective gasp-
ing in the room. It came at him from all angles.
And why not? He'd just made the largest bid of
the night, several thousand over estimate. At this
rate, Halcyone was certain to open its doors to
the public with tens of millions at its disposal.

"Going once. Going twice."

Bashir locked eyes with Yusra as he hit the
gavel. "Sold."

The auction wrapped up, he thanked his guests
for their generosity and walked offstage, and on
his way to his seat, he noticed that Yusra had
gotten up and disappeared just as dinner was
being served.

"Outside," Otis and Evgenia said, knowing
where Bashir wanted to be.

Yusra was sitting on a bench with a sea view.

"I don't know where to begin," he rasped, claiming the seat by her, and draping his arm over the back of the bench they shared.

Yusra's lips quirked into a teasing smile. "That was a staggering bid. Wasn't the whole point to get others to empty their pockets tonight, and not yours?"

"There was no way I would have let anyone walk away with that portrait."

"I'm sure that would make the artist happy to hear."

He stared at her, knowing he wasn't wrong when he said, "Then let me say this formally, so there's no misunderstanding—thank you. For the portrait. And for showing up and supporting this inaugural night."

Thank you for sticking by me.

Bashir didn't know if he stood a chance at having her around for longer, but he didn't want the sun rising on her not knowing that he loved her. It had been a love that had sneaked up on him. For so long, he had been cautious to give himself up to any emotion that could inflict harm on him. He had loved his family and Imran, and he lost all of them.

But I already lost Yusra these past few weeks.

And he would lose her forever if he allowed this reunion to slip him by.

Because he would rather have loved her than

have lost her. Both were an inescapable fate, but only one could give him a lifetime of happiness to experience and fondly remember.

"Did I ever tell you the myth of Halcyone?"

"No, I don't believe so," Yusra replied and leaned into him once his arm pulled down from the back of the bench and over her shoulders. "I like stories though."

Bashir's smile glowed down on her.

"Halcyone and Ceyx were a vainglorious couple who believed their love was as strong and powerful as that of Hera and Zeus, the queen and king of the gods. Angering Zeus, they were both killed. Ceyx while he was fishing the sea where he drowned, and Halcyone in her grief at losing her husband tossed herself into the very same sea after him."

"That's so sad."

"The gods thought so too. So, they resurrected them as a pair of halcyon birds. I always liked the story because it inspired hope in the bleakest of times. It's why I felt it was a fitting name for the nonprofit." Bashir squeezed her closer, turning so her hand and face rested on his chest. "I missed you. I shouldn't have walked away from you. It's a mistake that haunts me."

Yusra's eyes pricked at his kind words. They echoed her sentiments, but she was fearful to trust them too quickly. What if she was wrong again? Then nothing would have changed, and their marriage would be doomed to unhappiness. She erred on the side of caution, guarded her heart instead and quietly said, "I got your gift. The brushes were very thoughtful of you."

"I'm glad you put them to good use." Bashir paused. A dreaded beat lapsed and then, "You brought my family back to life again. I didn't think it was possible. And yet you made it so."

For a moment, her big, brooding husband sat quietly, his gaze drifting from her to the night-darkened sea. Finally, he said, "I went into this marriage, fully committed to the fact that it would be purely practical for us to raise our sons together. I wasn't in it for romance and love. I won't lie. Right from the beginning I was attracted to you. But I thought that was all it could be. Then the more I got to know you, the more my admiration and affection for you grew.

"Frankly speaking, it scared me. For so long I'd sealed off that part of me that knew how to love that I wasn't sure what to do about it. Even with my experience raising Zaire and being his father, it didn't prepare me for a whole family. For AJ.

"For you, Yusra." He looked at her, and she felt her jaws slacken at the emotion playing on his features. She spotted fear, remorse, anticipation, and beneath all three, the admiration for her he spoke of.

"You could have walked away at any point. Yet you took my calls, and you let me speak to the boys and you're here now. I'm just wondering what I did to deserve you when I've been nothing but a coward lately."

"I was scared too," she admitted and sought his hand, entwining their fingers together. "For so long, I had learned to believe that love wasn't trustworthy or steadfast. But I was wrong. I trust you with our children, and I trust and like myself when I'm with you, Bashir. You've supported my art. You have been nothing but kind and giving since I met you." She laughed softly and rubbed his long, thick curly beard. "Okay, maybe I could do with a little less brooding, but even that's not enough to diminish my faith in you and our marriage."

"I don't want to lose you," he breathed, his usual composure crumbling and panic looking out at her.

"I'm not leaving," she whispered with a smile.

Bashir sagged back against the bench, relief stark on his face. He closed his eyes and murmured, "Give me a second. Hearing you say that after longing for it—I need time to process."

She couldn't help the giggle that slipped free. He lazily opened his eyes and looked to her, a sexy smirk kicking up his mouth. His low laughter rumbled out slow and sweet. It fluttered over her skin, heating her from the outside in. And it lured her closer to him, enchanted by the way he was looking at her—like she meant the world to him.

Like I am *his world.*

That was all she needed to see to do what she wanted to from the beginning. Bashir had the same thought apparently as he leaned in and met her halfway.

Their kiss was an explosion of their combined need for each other. Pent-up frustration and yearning packed into thirty breathless seconds. Coming up for air was torture in its own way. She could have kissed him all night, and still not gotten enough.

Cradling her onto his lap, Bashir smoothed his hands down her back before wrapping his arms around her waist. He pecked her mouth. And in between kisses, he murmured, "I think I love you, Yusra Amin."

"You think?" She held him back with a hand to his chest; her eyebrows snapped up with an unspoken challenge, his lips kiss swollen and hers feeling equally and delightfully puffy from their display of affection. But she wouldn't be distracted. "Do you *think* or do you *know*?" Because there was a difference.

She *knew* she loved this man, to the living, healing, loving core of her.

Bashir laughed deeply. Closing his hand over hers on his chest, he spoke the words she wished to hear. "I love you, Yusra. I knew it when I ran away from you, and it might have taken me a while to admit it to myself, but I know now. Just as I know I won't ever stop loving you."

At that, her overjoyed laughter mingled with a sob or two, her cheeks home to a lot of happy tears. She hugged him tightly, her arms squeezing him closer, her heart impossibly full of the love she had for him. "I love you too," she laughed and cried at once. She drew back and covered him in kisses, moaning against his mouth, "You taste sweet," when he teased past her lips and explored her more intimately.

"It's *soumada*. I'll get you to taste some later."

She didn't want anything else but him right now. And she showed him with more affectionate caresses and kisses.

They might have stayed like that all night too—just as she wished, but a score of bright lights illuminated over the sea. She stared in shock as a swarm of multicolored lights spiraled in time with each other through the air. Squinting, she thought she saw…

"Drones?" she said in giddy wonder at the fireworks show without the pyrotechnics. Hundreds of the small, unmanned vehicles took to the air and began a coordinated synchronized show of kaleidoscopic lights.

"Ah, that would be my surprise. I found another use for the drones, now that Project Halcyone's construction is done." He regarded his expensive watch and hummed approvingly. "Good, they're perfectly timed."

And almost as perfectly, the sound of children's laughter floated over to where they were seated. "Is that…?"

A nod and grin from Bashir confirmed it. "The boys seem to have found us."

Yusra had all but a minute to scramble off Bashir's lap and straighten herself out. He smoothed his rumpled dress shirt and dinner jacket and straightened his crooked bow tie.

Alcina and Nadim carried the boys to them, leaving as soon as Yusra and Bashir had Zaire and AJ in their care.

Zaire hugged her, and AJ snuggled Bashir. Smiling over at each other, Bashir brushed her hand and she slid her palm into his. Together, they looked out over the sea where the unmanned drones created prismatic shapes and figures, their family complete and wondrously perfect.

And to think an accidental baby swap had brought them all of this.

EPILOGUE

A week later

"Happy birthday!"

Amidst the congratulatory cheers, Yusra mimed blowing out the candles to show her newly minted three-year-old sons exactly how to do it. But even with their impressive attempts, AJ and Zaire couldn't blow out the flames on their jungle-themed chocolate cake. Bashir came to their rescue. He sneakily huffed at the cake, and *whoosh.* the candles were snuffed.

Everyone clapped and the birthday boys beamed at the attention they were getting.

Someone flicked the lights back on, and the cake was served. But not before Yusra and Bashir snapped family photos with their children.

"You're not smiling in this one," she said after seeing how the photo turned out. She tsked up a her husband. "We have to take it again."

Bashir waited until the first flash went off on the camera phone.

He then leaned down and kissed her on the cheek.

His hand slid discreetly from the small of her back to brush her backside. A flash went off just as her eyes widened and she snapped her head to him. She batted his hand away before he could weaken her knees any more than he already had. Ever since they had fully consummated their marriage, he had been even more insatiable than usual.

"I couldn't help myself," he said cheekily. But she couldn't take his apology seriously when his eyes twinkled mischievously. And before she could half-heartedly scold him, he scooped up Zaire and AJ and hurried away from her, back to their guests in a room festooned with yellow, green and brown balloons and streamers, potted palm trees and even an inflatable round pool filled with sand and beach toys. Bashir had wanted to bring in chimpanzees for the jungle-themed birthday party, but she'd talked him out of it. There would be enough to keep the boys occupied. They were only three, after all.

Despite anticipating leaving Greece once Bashir had successfully launched his nonprofit, Project Halcyone, they were still living at the villa in Zákynthos. After some discussion, she and Bashir decided to stay there for a little while longer. Their boys liked the tranquil island, and so did she. Eventually they would return to Uganda and finally look into purchasing a home together for their family. And she had one more reason to look forward to going back now: her art was being showcased in her friend Samira's gallery. Yusra had finally braved asking her friend to review her work, and it was like Bashir had said, Samira had immediately jumped on inviting her to join her upcoming, buzzy exhibition. Yusra would be one of many African artists showcased, and she couldn't think of a better way to celebrate her return to her art.

As the party wound down, Yusra began clearing up, but she paused to take a look around the room full of their friends and family. Otis and Evgenia, Nadim and Alcina, and others who had come to celebrate the day with her and Bashir and their family. She looked over to the projector screens, recalling them from her wedding day. This time they hadn't just been used to include her parents and siblings, but Bashir's aunt, uncle and many cousins in Somalia as well. Bashir had invited them virtually after finally reconnecting with the family he'd thought he had lost when he ran away from them.

She knew how hard it was for him to revisit the past, but he had done it for the sake of their children.

And he reminded her again when he found

her alone in the kitchen after the gifts were unwrapped and the boys were left to play with their
many new toys.

"Did you have a good time?" he asked and
turned her to face him gently.

She pressed her hands to his taut abs. "I was
just about to ask you the same thing."

"I did. The best part was having our families
meet. I think my aunt and your mother will get
along thick as thieves, and your father and my
uncle will likely continue that spirited discussion
of theirs on which is better—a coastal city or a
country farm. Though I will say when we finally
all are in one room together, they might be a bit
too much to handle."

Yusra snorted laughter. And then she sighed
blissfully and hugged him. "I love this for you."

"I love it for *us*. The boys should have all the
family they can get. It's something I missed, but
I don't want them to have the same past as me."
He rubbed her back and embraced her closer. "I
wouldn't have any of this without you."

"Me?" she squeaked up at him, shocked. "What
did I do?"

Bashir gazed down at her, his eyes searching,
probing. Then seemingly finding what he wanted
in her, he huskily said, "I always thought I was
happier alone. And then I met you. I forgot how

good it felt to be loved, and now I also know what it means to be *in* love."

Yusra couldn't have agreed more.

* * * * *

If you enjoyed this story, check out these other great reads from Hana Sheik

Forbidden Kisses with Her Millionaire Boss
Temptation in Istanbul
Second Chance to Wear His Ring

All available now!